Tila Lake

Tila Lake

Tolulope Kode

Matador
Unit E2 Airfield Business Park,
Harrison Road, Market Harborough,
Leicestershire. LE16 7UL
Tel: 0116 2792299
Email: books@troubador.co.uk
Web: www.troubador.co.uk/matador
Twitter: @matadorbooks

ISBN 978 1805140 481

British Library Cataloguing in Publication Data.
A catalogue record for this book is available from the British Library.

Printed and bound in Great Britain by 4edge Limited
Typeset in 14pt Adobe Garamond Pro by Troubador Publishing Ltd, Leicester, UK

Matador is an imprint of Troubador Publishing Ltd

A Note on References

I found *The Biu Book*: *A Collection and Reference Book on Biu Division (Northern Nigeria); 1954-1956*; author, J. G Davies, a relevant text in preliminary research on Biu culture.

All conversations between characters in this book are entirely fictional.

PART ONE

I

Children dashed along the streets while cows came thumping along. No trace of mechanised farming here. Yet you saw rows of full-blown maize neatly arranged on their farms. *Tuwo masara* is the staple food here; it is made of maize. There were no motorbikes to transport the harvested maize to the houses. But it was delivered by a chain of people waiting for it to be harvested. Little commuting was done here, which means the villages, though scattered, operated as one unit.

You could tell the extent of civilisation in these parts from the beauty of asymmetric designs. Treetop and V-shaped roofs allowed more air ventilation from the sides. As with the exchange of ideas between distinct features in designs. Some of these designs were of the Bura fashion.

It may seem that the asymmetric designs alter as one moves through the villages, such that new Babur ones can spring forth from the standard Bura designs.

Their livelihood was exposed by the various dispatches of people buying and selling. Those who hawked essentials from street to street and house to house. While others were gathered for other communal purposes. It was easy to tell the daily commuters from the slow walkers who plied the same routes.

Inspecting each village by their compounds. The weavings on the thatch roofs. The number of children playing in the sand. What are they playing at? They are making some sketches. What are these things? The *sketches* disperse in various directions.

The children bore the marks as *sketches*, so they did not go astray. The *sketches* were emblems and flowed like a river wherever it pleases. Speak to the river; say what you desire from it. It first must be appeased. The crocodile did so by its many tumbling. Where will I find such a river? My burden on it I lay to carry away.

The children could be heard singing as their fortunes were directed. They marched on as before without the sounds of drums. What did the drums say? Who was the drummer? The one sighted at a distance where the sound came from. So, proceed further on, as our fortunes direct. There was a gathering as the melody gathered momentum. They were well accustomed to such tidings by the river or at its banks, where some respite came.

We followed the river to where it offloaded its banks. At Tila Lake, the river formed emblems. In this sketch, there were crocodiles about a lake stretched... We saw people gathered as if they were about to make some consultation.

We followed the river's twists. The river glided over rocks, into pebbles. On excavating the pebbles, we found crocodile remains.

Were the children messengers? Did the children also point to the one atop a tree? The one atop the tree was also a child. That was why children were gathered there. This must be some playground for children. When we approached them, they reappeared in twos, then in threes, and made the same sketches.

The children soon came to bear the burden of religion.

When poverty ravages the land, all aspects are affected.

It is like a scorching fire that turns the green grass brown.

The *Almajiri*.

2

On just one circle of Miringa soil, laid houses and stalls—to name a few—allowing the streets to pass between them. This circle spread its tentacles to other areas in Miringa and was wrapped up in Biu Local Government. The streets could otherwise be called passages, except for one major road that led one from the Miringa bus stop to the main market area, which suddenly became boisterous at about 10 am. It was indeed a day everyone had been waiting for. Stall owners had now moved from their usual positions to other sections in the main market area. Their faces were lit up in anticipation as they expected their customers to patronise them. They were consoled because prospective customers expected the best goods and services on market days. A passer-by was lured into patronising the stalls because he was a prospective customer. The excitement in the air was beyond the selling or buying. It stemmed from virtually the entire village converging on this spot. We mingled, and our minds were taken off in a moment from the main purpose of gathering as we met familiar faces.

But the tempo of activities at Miringa seemed to reduce on other days. The people had now dispersed and were back in their stalls, which ran side by side through the houses. However, it was a different ball game when the rains came. It interrupted their long work hours at the stalls. This time everyone went about with hoes and cutlasses, and would usually hang the former on his shoulders when returning from the farm.

In the past, Biu indigenes did not have to trek several kilometres to the farm. Their farms were right under their noses. Some lived in the mountains. It's amazing how they survived the dramatic climate over there. That could be trivial since the terrain was favourable to farming and hunting of stray animals who wandered into the waiting hands of the people.

We still have settlers around the base of Gwaram mountain in Gwaram village. The other mountains in Biu served as a picturesque expression. Such mountains certainly affected the extreme cold temperatures one saw during the harmattan. It seemed even colder when I heard the high-pitched voices of the *Almajiris* reciting Arabic letterings at my doorstep at about 5 am. I was probably struggling to keep still or was still, and would not even entertain the thought of moving a leg or an arm, for I thought that would invite cold. However, at the sound of their voices, I moved on impulse.

Are these flesh and blood? I wondered and tried to assume my initial position. When I peeped over the aluminium fence later in the morning, there they were—in the cold! A boy was beaten because he missed one of the Arabic verses. The boy simply carried his slate, which fell beside the fire made to keep them warm, and continued with the ritual. They screamed out those verses as if their lives depended on them. And one could not help but think they were beaten occasionally because they did not scream loud enough.

The *Almajiris* later roamed the streets in search of their daily bread. I could not help but feel sympathy when my eyes fell on several of them, scrambling for some *kose* tossed to the ground. This was after they waited hopelessly, watching others who had been eating. The seller sometimes felt pity for them and put some *kose* onto one plate they carried. The *bearer* carried the plate to a safe place, but before he could get to his desired destination, the plate's contents were shared voraciously among the lucky ones.

It is doubtful if the indigenes were particularly emotional about the plight of the *Almajiri*—as I was—though they had to give them food. They believed in their prayers. I rarely paid attention to these prayers, though I usually gave them food until one Alhaji drew my attention to their mumbling. It is believed that the prayers had a thorough way to heaven.

There was relative calm during the market activities. Where people approached from far and near, giving exchanges in salutary messages. On market days, they did lots of exchanges for economic benefits. Each was a test of bargaining power. Like a wrestling contest. It was a recreation. They seemed subconsciously aware of the economic effect. They mimed folklore while anticipating a customer. Miming such folklore in the market brought enormous energy as they were promised goodwill. It would have drawn some customers to them—who recalled such.

The advantage they sought. Market days were a pastime.

The market was a melting pot of cultural exchanges and traditions. Here, all the rumours were dispelled. A witch flying on a broomstick is a fairy tale—yet it is regarded as a cultural exchange. Folklore has been revived. It was said that Madika flew on a broomstick to her abode in the woods. She screamed as she went. Her voice pitched high like a bird's. *If you want to see her, buy this gel and rub it into your eyes.* The kids were pulling their parents to the scenes of a performance where a man performed magic. A broomstick was bent and weaved into a mat that beat waves of air about.

"Madika danced on the broomstick like this," the man showed with a dancing broomstick. He wove a mat from other broomsticks. He presented the mat to a boy. "You can buy this mat for 100 naira," said the man.

The boy sent the mat to the ground and beat the waves out of the mat.

"Tap it from both sides, little magician. Would you also want to leave for the woods?" The seller asked, referencing Madika's sojourn to the woods.

"I love adventure," replied the boy.

"Madika had to find her climate for magic. I

come from Shani and perform here on Sundays," the seller said.

"Does magic have anything to do with the place it is performed?"

"We smell the air and conjure. The tricks of magic change with the place. It takes a while to perform after a process of habitation. Then you can learn to meditate," he replied.

"I come from far and near." He called out to the puzzlement of those around. They turned around to see him, but looked back at their purchase.

The vigour, perseverance, and niceties were on display. From there, the people gathered were dispersed.

The market system made it easier for those working in offices to relate to the anticipations of artisans, traders, and farmers. The farmers might have expected interest rates similar to the spread of their crops. This anticipation might have been informed by a trade and barter system. Their fathers ploughed the ground to produce enough grains and milked cows for sufficient *madara*. This was given to the women to sell and make a profit. The men sold *nama*. Each household had domesticated animals according to the number of children. For chiefs and village heads that performed rites on behalf of the community, there was a quota from a system of returns, calculated by rotation of market days. The chiefs and village heads were also responsible for the redistribution of these returns—as with trading in the market.

They were gathered here in anticipation of returns following the ploughing of the previous seasons. The performance of rites came before the distribution of returns. Once these shifted positions, so did the returns. It was automatic. Once the rites were lost, a sense of distribution was lost. Of the returns. Giving rise to chaos and confusion. Artificial means of distribution couldn't make redistribution. Of the returns.

They asked themselves how much work would generate a plentiful yield—given variables such as climate and soil conditions. They were soon disappointed, given the current economics of trade. Their frustrations were about these variables. Hence, their case was inexplicable. They might have been swindled by the Nigerian government. Even the Nigerian government is being swindled by its international partners. When will Nigeria be free from the debt of accrued loans?

The economists knew the volume of assets churned out per financial quarter. This was because they had active representatives in the market. They made a forecast of revenue and expenditure—considering liquidity, which was thought to be satisfactory. This was done to balance their accounts. Yet they expected customer-related issues in banks—and at the secretariat. The customers were keen to receive their proceeds, but queues hindered them. When they just came back tired from work, they assumed the bankers would easily relate to their plight. But there was a delay in cash flows despite a computerised system. The situation was not much different in cities—there were only false hopes.

3

Certain Biu persons witnessed the birth of Tila Lake. They were present at its very inception. All were stationed around the lake at the time the crater gave way, leading to the lake's formation. The people were thought dead, as the force had propelled them into oblivion. Now it was homecoming. The same people have gathered again. Some had been reborn into other persons throughout the eras. But on hearing about the predicament of Tila Lake, their instincts reawakened, bringing them to form a committee.

Though they were propelled by unknown forces, they were brought back to Tila Lake's *perimeter*. They could go no further. A spring of a well was formed around the sides of the crater, bringing their quest to a close. All those who were reborn could vividly recall the birth of the lake. Going further from where they stood, there was vegetation; even trees where birds kept their nests. It must have been from one of these eggs that this creature, which resembled a bird, was hatched. It repelled the people, creating its *perimeter*. Again, there were some trees and vegetation. Because it sensed that these people were about to write history, the creature emerged on the scene. Waving its tail to prevent them from coming closer.

"What is in that well of water?" someone asked.

"What is this creature doing here?" asked another.

To understand the essence of the lake is to understand the essence of the creature. But the bird creature was not within reach. How would you negotiate with this creature? They left the scene, only to return the next day to see crocodiles in the lake. They could see their gaping mouths from a distance as the crocodiles swarmed against each other.

"That's interesting. The lake was formed because of the crocodiles?" an observer puzzled. "What activities would go on here?"

This seems to be a centre of attraction. But they wouldn't know what activities were performed there until everyone in the village realised this mysterious lake. With little ado, the news spread around all villages. Everyone couldn't witness the crocodiles all at once. So, a committee was formed to organise trips to the lake.

There was excitement in Biu for the next 11 days. This one event united all and sundry. It was visible in the expressions on their faces when they met during market days. However, their excitement was soon short-lived, as they realised they couldn't go beyond the *perimeter*. The bird creature was always present to keep them at bay.

Looking at the appearance of the bird creature, they knew it wasn't something they would combat. Soon they discovered the creature confined itself to a mound. Its demeanour was sad now. No one knew what its expectations were. Some wished it would fly into oblivion or one tree nearby.

"Perhaps this creature demands some respect. It seems to know more about the lake than we do. We are gearing up for surprises if we come closer to the lake," an observer noted.

The *perimeter's* line seemed to weaken when the creature was not in sight. Keen observers noticed the creature disappeared through a mound, only to appear again. So, the people felt even more comfortable moving closer till they got to the nearest likely point. Now it was noted that the creature seldom appeared. They soon forgot about its existence and visited the lake at will. But they were concerned about their safety as the crocodiles grew in number.

"But just a while ago, we were itching to see the lake. Now that the *perimeter* is removed, we are sceptical of going further," they reasoned among themselves.

"Could the bird creature have empowered the crocodiles?"

"That is antithetical to natural laws. Crocodiles feed on birds. How would that be possible?"

"Such thinking will not bring us anywhere close to the answer. How would you interact with the crocodiles?"

"Why do we need to?"

"We need to understand the laws that govern this place; otherwise, we are taking a risk with our frequent visits. Maybe we need to take a clue from the bird creature and visit less often."

"The business here is more serious than we think."

"But you know caution is of importance here."

The lake would reveal itself. First, it reflected

surfaces through which people visualised their images. But the images were many; they even included some people who were not present. Tila Lake had taken the recordings of everyone in Biu. They could, therefore, understand even deeper matters from the lake. The lake showed the paths each of them had taken. They came to the lake from time to time for their paths to remain engraved.

Although they had seen the creature initially, there wasn't any record of further encounters. It seemed the creature was happy with this arrangement.

A *bearer* would always come in a procession and carry out his duties. The Emir of Biu was happy—so was everyone else. As time went on, the creature showed again an expression of sadness when the people tried to edge in the *perimeter*. This was recorded, but it is doubtful if it was taken seriously, as no more references were made.

The appearance of the bird creature provoked enquiries about Tila Lake. Tila Lake is in Southwest Biu, stretching from Kwaya, Jera, and Hinna environs. You must have heard of Tila Lake. Tila Lake makes the land green, as its water runs underneath through tunnel spaces.

Some of these drained away and found their way past vegetation and into some collection.

A conservationist was there collecting this water, yet he was unseen. With these, he wet some plants, now grown into mighty trees where birds had their nests. This place quaked with strange sounds. The trees blossomed. The land became merry.

Tila Lake was a spot for tourists and *lovers*. Here, secrets were waiting to be uncovered, glistering water filled with crocodiles. Events that trail civilisation came as a disguise.

From its inception, it was a crater—then Tila Lake was formed. Sparks of this crater were kept by custodians for the maintenance of Tila Lake. The crocodiles were now in open view. And kept alive till they were buried in the sparks. Because no two things are the same. Prove it then, if you may. But now the sparks provided the glitter and paths through which the crocodiles glowed. This provided a system of synchronicity. Or harmony between two *classes*.

The birth of Tila Lake brought reflections of events like waves in a pool that could be traced to infinity. Rather than worry about what is in the firm grip of history, we should investigate Tila Lake, which is the centre of controversy. And recourse to the solutions—when the villages are in turmoil because the people have lost grip on the essence of the lake.

There was a celebration at the birth of Tila Lake. When the crater exploded, and its surfaces were formed, some watched the slits within the centre of gravity and puzzled at it. What was causing the ground to give way? The well of spring water emerged after several layers of earth were displayed off the surface. What a sight to behold. They hid behind trees so they could catch glimpses of the event. Then the bird creature appeared from a mound and cleared the stones and soil—even uprooting certain roots that were growing from the sides of the lake.

The water was believed to be free from chemicals, as the threat of plants dying was taken away. Crocodiles from the earth emerged to walk towards the water. It seemed they were going to have a bath. The water was muddy from the mix of soil remains and water. Once again, the bird creature came to hand-pick the soil, leaving the glistering water. The glistering water formed bubbles of higher temperature. Now you could see the eyes of the crocodiles distinctly. Even those behind the trees could feel their gaze—as they tried to catch glimpses of the lake. Each connecting glimpse formed different crocodile patterns. The crocodiles were known to them.

They were there at the lake's formation. The bird creature could perceive every movement around the *perimeter* of the lake as they moved behind the trees. Sometimes the creature would come close to the trees, growing suspicious of the movements. She now seemed like a guard who watched the lake for 24 hours. What could provoke the appearance of the bird creature? Strange movements, it seemed, which were unknown to Tila Lake. The bird creature disappeared into the mound just as she came out of it. The observers resurfaced from hiding; surveyed the lake and went back into hiding, just as before.

Questions continued to trail the creature's first appearance at the formation of Tila Lake. We know now that the bird creature had been seen handpicking the sand and roots of trees to leave the glistering water of Tila Lake. Such purified water was required for Tila Lake. The creature must have created the *perimeter* to control the visits to the lake. Such a barrier the *bearer* had to cross to gain access to the purified water. If the bird creature was pleased, it would permit entry to the *bearer*.

The *bearer* prowled the barricade. The *bearer* performed priest-like functions. Rites characterised his outings at the barricade about Tila Lake. A maiden sang at her courtyard at some perceivable distance from the *perimeter*. The maiden continued her dance, but suspiciously this time. There were a lot of sleeper crocodiles than usual at such an hour. A gong was sounded for alertness. But they slumbered. Those who had smelled some danger coming. But like sleepy crocodiles, they lay optimistically, expecting the enemy might swat like an encroaching fly in front of them. Instead, they were taken from behind and had to bail themselves out first, before any other.

The river girl was bait for the unsuspecting *bearer*—to watch him when he came close. She often passed the *perimeter* to the stream. A lake filled with crocodiles. The *bearer* peered through the holes to watch a maiden perform some rituals.

The girl moved out when she heard the sound of drums. The girl who danced by the river. The drum sounded like war. Who beats these drums? Men of valour. By the magical drums, she lured the *bearer* to sleep. The river girl conjured the rhythm of Tila Lake's waters. The *bearer* was intoxicated by the sound of drums, as its rhythm mixed with flowing water from Tila Lake. He had once forgotten his aim, and no longer had the valour of men.

The *bearer* was tasked with performing rites to forestall such security breaches. The *bearer* was heading to perform rites to reconstruct the barricade to fence Tila Lake in, so its water did not drain away. Following a successful outing, the *bearer* would invoke the spirit of the crocodiles to begin festivities.

But once he began his ritual, the river girl emerged from the water and stood in his way. She created pathways of water flow. Two crocodiles followed and blocked the pathways. The river wouldn't flow. Its custodian needed to be appeased.

"Why obstruct my mission here?" the *bearer* queried.

"I can see your proficiency in the *works of Moses, as with the parting of the Red Sea*. Do you have any of his scrolls there?" the bearer questioned.

"Why would you bother? A *bearer* must find his way regardless of the obstacles," the river girl replied.

Fighting began between the *bearer* and the river girl, whereupon the river girl summoned guards at the ready. *The bearer was close enough to draw the attention of the guards, who stood at the ready.* She signalled an echo towards them from afar.

The place looked deserted. They trod the paths with caution. There were among them spies with three eyes and scratches all over their faces as masks for disguise. There were scratches all over the faces of the assailants. The invaders came in disguise. But their masks were being unveiled.

They began firing arrows so that the barricade gave way. Spears flew in the *bearer's* direction. Some formed holes in the barricade. The invaders' arrows were coming swiftly through the barricade. The arrows were gliding between alternating trees and piercing through unsuspecting hearts.

A spear just caught someone. The spear was poisoned. How would he recover? The dying one was taken to the medicine man, so he could. That killed faster than you think. The spears were wielded to keep as much poison as possible for the target. The defences were now broken. Just then, the *bearer* found a dying man who the spear had caught. Then others.

The invaders were familiar with the unfamiliar terrains, having experimented with such previously. Their strikes were perfect. They had a strategy and would beat any team frontally.

The barricade had broken down. The *bearer* was denied access to the sacred crocodiles, which he required to perform the rituals. Alas, his hopes for commencing with festivities were dashed in quick succession.

When the enemy breaks through the barricade and steals from what was within. Exposing the most vulnerable. Their cries were all over the villages until they reached distant lands.

Repairs needed to be made to the barricade fencing at Tila Lake. The *bearer* thus sought a way to begin with the rites. An invasion was becoming more and more likely as the barricade to the marketplaces had been broken.

The hinges of the barricade shook violently as the river girl escaped. She escaped through the loosened hinges thanks to the agitations of the prisoners. She had escaped once her mission was completed. And flowed like a river to Tila Lake. The barricade was transformed into a tunnel that allowed gushing water to flow.

Water held up gushed out of the tunnel holes, flowing into marketplaces. The water overflowed its banks into the marketplaces as it swept away boxes of potash and salt waiting to be sold. These were diverted away from conventional trade routes, as they were siphoned off the source of production.

There was chaos. Tables were upturned and boxes of money were carted away. Even jewellery and some priceless artefacts were on display. Whose origins could be traced to faraway lands. The paths traced to other explorers who had come defeated. The invader saw what the indigenous people of Biu traded among themselves.

Arrowhead shells were picked off the ground. Shells of granite were found ashore. Some others settled on the ground. The encircled spears formed a pattern like a battle formation. This showed the assailant was close by. Those working at the site were puzzled by the development.

Economic activities had come to a standstill. Far way up the hills of Biu was a scenery of mashed-up farmlands. Donkeys were a rare sight. Hundreds of cattle were carted away. Seeing that there was no one to tend to them. Their way of life had been disrupted. Some lands were still up for grabs and thus allocated to certain families. Other concessions were made to ease the process of recovery.

The crocodile on the Emir's flag glowed as you came near. It must be one of those in Tila Lake. The radiation spread across the room, which enveloped the visitor in an embrace. Tilted behind the curtains, ongoing scenes were kept away. A constant ritual was underway.

What is this crocodile in a palace? The man who walked into the palace tried to recall. He was a known hunter and must have encountered many crocodiles. He won many wrestling contests. Fought with beasts, yet walked out unharmed. He had walked around the villages chanting, making shows to the bemusement of the villages. When they gathered around him, he made a fire with his hands, keeping all warm and secure. It was foretold that he must do so.

The emir sat, paying no attention to the visitor's dilemma, even though he was now visibly worried. The news of the invasion had reached the Emir. Many *bearers* had come and gone. But the one with a quest would make his way to Tila Lake and unravel what was behind the glow. *The bearer* must yet make some connection regarding the essence of the glow. This was his first hurdle in the journey.

"*Bundi Alvari*," the visitor called out to the Emir.

"The Emir greets you," was the reply.

The *bearer* walked in to report on his findings at Tila Lake. He was supposed to perform rites at the lake. The Emir was startled at his findings.

The *bearer* could not begin with the construction of the barricade as with the rites.

Such events sometimes intercepted meetings at the palace. Just as the Emir was drawn to a commotion around the Lake some years ago. The *bearer's* image was projected from Tila Lake to the palace. The Emir had sensed the *bearer's* dilemma and hesitated while the meeting was ongoing.

"You must go to Tila Lake at once." A sense of urgency dawned on him. "The barricade must be repaired," he continued. "Also, bring for me some of the water you collect so that we may continue further rituals. The crocodile is now known to you that you may return safely. Only now it is docile. Take care, you do not miss the time."

The *bearer's* mission was known to the Emir. As the flashing points continued, the *bearer* was asked to concentrate on Tila Lake to understand the quest at hand. The *bearer* sought to merge the flashing points and focus them toward Tila Lake—like a cannonball. He had to ensure it didn't spiral out of control and create other flashing points. Tila Lake was the destination of the cannonball. To dissolve in it and birth the lake anew.

"Nice try," said the Emir. "The flashing points have been reduced to three. If these were merged, it would yet create three directions for the cannonball."

"My hands are slipping from them. I need to get a proper grip," said the *bearer*.

"Very well then, keep trying. You get better with the number of tries, allowing you to refocus your energies."

"I know I have to do this for Biu. We must regain control of Tila Lake's *perimeter*. There have not been visits to Tila Lake lately. I understand the essence of this ritual."

The Emir sat comfortably in his chair once this ritual was successfully carried out. With his emissaries gathered about him. At that moment, their anticipations ran high. A sense of calm returned on the completion of the ritual. Only then visitors were allowed in again with their myriad of issues, which were submitted and logged by the Emir's secretary.

Drowning voices called from the deep of Tila Lake as the *bearer* hastened his footsteps. He knew it was time. At once, he began shouting as he left the palace. "I am the one who leads the way to Tila Lake." A glow appeared from the torch on his head—leading the way. That was a confirmation of scaling the first hurdle.

"I am the chosen one to clear the way," he cried. Just as he stepped out of the palace, a *dogari* paved the way. He had the foresight of the trial that awaited him on the journey. He alerted the spirits, who were waiting to accept his sacrifice. His communication thus began.

There were admirers of the sights at the lake. Those who were privy to the *bearer's* encounter at the palace referred to the glow from the crocodile when they saw one. Others were simply puzzled and enquired about the associated incidents. Their experiences were complementary, giving birth to new ones. These awakened the sense of rituals in the community. The rites were borne out of the rituals. The *bearer* must be known to the crocodile if he successfully carried out these rites. That was the essence of the disruption of his journey, and the two crocodiles sent his way. But now his journey was set.

The *bearer* made headway with the help of his torch. He hurried past several people on the way to Tila Lake. The twigs on both sides of the path wouldn't deter him—unhappy faces wouldn't either. Approaching a forked road, he thought of those he met on the way. He would have asked for directions, but they were far off. He could barely see the baskets on their heads. However, he pressed on. "It's a rocky path from here," he remembered. Suddenly, his torch dimmed. He could no longer see the way.

It is assumed he was known to the crocodile or vice versa. But he wasn't. Something had gone wrong.

The *bearer* was now searching for a cannonball. The cannonball was a roll of fire from the crater borne out of the sparks of crocodiles. He knew the cannonball was somewhere around. The prospect of a rebirth at Tila Lake was diminishing. Life in the lake was turbulent, and the tensions were high as village heads awaited a successful outing. There were chances the cannonball could spiral out of control if it wasn't dissolved in the lake. Then a rescue team would be in operation.

"It seems early to consider such permutations. Let's be optimistic," said one.

"But we also have to be time conscious if there is a need to salvage the situation," said another.

"I know. It rarely gets to this. Once a *bearer* leaves the palace, it is almost certain his outing is successful."

"Is there a way to trace his location from the palace?"

"You might trace the location of the *bearer*, but I am not sure if you can do so with the cannonball.

Remember, the cannonball was dispelled before the *bearer* began his journey. Even the fears of the journey were so dispelled."

"It seems the *bearer* is the only one who can get us out of this quagmire."

"Remember, that is why he is called the *bearer*. He might try reversing his actions if that option is open to him."

They were unaware that the situation was more severe. The *bearer* would have communicated his concerns, but he had lost his torch. If he didn't get to Tila Lake in time, the cannonball would engulf the entire place. Some had come and suffered a similar fate. In other cases, the cannonball would simply roll away, dissipating its energy. Since he had directed the cannonball, he had the power to stop a potential explosion. But he needed to revive the crocodiles, the essence of the ritual.

After a few steps to his right, he got to a swamp. *This can't be the place*, he thought. But there were freshly made tracks scattered across the place. His fears were confirmed. The crocodiles had walked away.

Tila Lake had lost all its savour, and much debris clung to its sides. It had been unguarded for a while. Its gates were open to strangers, and much evil. The once glittering water was now murky. All was not well.

"Am I at Tila Lake?" he wondered.

As if to acknowledge his presence, some pelagic fish bubbled to the surface. Looking at them disinterestedly, he tried to connect with his fathers. He could hear their drowning voices as one aroused from sleep.

It was believed the *bearer* could not access Tila Lake because of the *perimeter* which formed a gulf. The creature appeared to establish authority over Tila Lake using the *perimeter*. Many years ago, the bird creature bore a resemblance to a woman aggrieved by excavators about the lake. Through many years, she had been half-transformed into a bird. Hence, her ancestry could not be established. Ironically, this meant she would not be appeased.

Thus, festivities had become non-existent, just as the bird creature had predicted. The Emir of Biu had been stripped of any following. The authority of the Emir over Tila Lake was called to question. The Emir sought other means of control besides the *perimeter*.

The elders assessed the opening of the gulf. The gulf formed the *perimeter* of Tila Lake. The bird creature emerged from this gulf, taking hold of the *perimeter*. The gulf widened, causing the *perimeter* to advance. Other times, the *perimeter* was retreating.

The history of the crater was in question. Beneath the crater, a mass of skeletons was found. Forensics shows the skeletons of a bird-like creature. The mass was gathered from a bird species, and, in fact, from one, not many. It was interesting to find oil dripping from the skeletons, proving many years of compression beneath the earth. But why had the mass risen to the surface?

Environmentalists were concerned about the effects of such a mass. Someone joked that "They could make a bonfire out of this pit of hell." It must have stirred religiosity in some causing debates. Perhaps Moses' scroll burnt along with this, too. The pit led into a cave where dark practices linger.

The chiefs needed to agree on the date of the finds to determine what use Tila Lake would be. Would the bird creature be of much significance if you couldn't separate the oil from the mass? If you could, to what extent would the creature be significant? Little did they know that there was burning underneath the mass within the depths of Tila Lake.

4

The *bearer* had yet to arrive. The prospect of constructing the barricade was dwindling. There was pandemonium everywhere—a feeling of loss. The people scattered everywhere in search of the *bearer*, who was their only hope of reviving their economic activities on market days. Had Tila Lake overflowed its banks, spilling unwholesomeness everywhere?

Tila Lake could not be reborn. When recreational activities were gone, there was little bargaining power to fuel the activities during market days. When would the tide of Tila Lake transport good tidings back and forth?

The gossip had turned unsavoury. But the clowns allowed good gossip. Out of such motivations, their activities produced streams of income.

The clowns were tasked with reporting these events from door to door. They were a recognised publicity group. Hence, they readily gained access to offices, outlets, and persons of interest. The clowns had been meeting with the village heads, one after the other. Especially those they felt were politically connected. Because the town was in disarray, the clowns met them randomly, with little notice.

The clowns caused some shivers down their spines. "This is no interview, but some investigation on a crime not committed," some politician had remarked. Clowns were the best interviewers. They were subtle. They came unnoticed and appeared to draw much attention when leaving. Here is a transcript of such an interview:

Please, sir, we took notice of your address some time ago. Though it was a while ago, we believe the subject of discussion is still much more relevant today. We have had pandemonium in the past, where everyone abruptly left the marketplace. On this ocassion, the distribution of goods and services ceased, because there was a little recreation in these activities. I will expatiate. The attraction that made us gather suddenly ceased. The same repelled us into our remote places.

Our rivers are contaminated. The children drink from such waters—they are falling sick. Someone attends to a child shivering with a fever. Doctors extract juice from plucked leaves to revive the child. The entire village is gathered to watch the event. The child dies. What happened to the child the previous day? The child had been seen bubbling. And the doctor had been seen to revive another the previous day. It didn't always have to be such a scene, but the villagers have now gathered for the wrong reasons. To watch infirmity plague the land. Where are the elders in the villages?

I recall vividly how the extract worked wrongly for the child. We called health to his weak bones. All to no avail. When all seemed to work. The villagers had been gathering to watch the debacle, maybe there could be one among them to revive the boy. The spark we get from our meetings is gone. If our activities were healthy as before, the boy could have been revived just by being amid them.

"Is that what you understand by recreation?" a village head asked the clowns.

"The essence of health is to recreate lost energies. We do this to remain healthy. Going to the medicine man is the last resort. Even our political activities are not healthy. Our politicians are bandits and criminals. They seek wealth through unscrupulous means. That's why there are killings during elections. It speaks volumes of the process and outcomes."

"Is that why they can't deliver on their promises once elected into office?"

"They can't because they haven't passed through the requisite screening process, just like the *bearer* couldn't enter Tila Lake. Those elected into these offices are mere ceremonial figures. It is as good as the *bearer* fetching water from some river and bringing it to the palace for the rituals."

"The rites performed by the *bearer* were important. There's a fine line between good and evil, and his outing's outcome highlights it. The *bearer's* plight was so surreal. A lot has been attributed to his journey."

"Is that also why rites come before the distribution of returns?"

"As we have seen, the activities at the market are now in disarray. People are now gathered to count their losses. Our politics is in disarray. Those foolish politicians think they can gain wealth by stealing."

"But they gain wealth."

"Why are they still stealing? It is a vicious circle that needs an exit loop before they can know true abundance. The land is famished, yet they milk it. The land is gracious. It produces milk but from famished hands. The hands beg for revival. They look the other way, and it swallows them up. That marks the end. What is the gain thereof?"

Now the people had come from other villages to sell their wares. But they were unfamiliar to their customers. Or approached them strangely, without prior motivations. It was unusual. Spies had infiltrated the market. The spies often peered through the holes in the barricade to give them a chance on the security guard-made watch. The spies could be identified by their tattoos.

There were spies and guards alike—court messengers. The guards watched out for spies among them, so they were suspicious when someone sneaked in through the barricade.

Madika was here like any other. Scanning the combative scenes on the barricade as if to bring it to life. A spy watched her as she brought the mural close. Madika had such inklings, but couldn't place where; she was in isolation, wanting freedom. She was curious about the announcement made about the river girl. Was she dead?

Madika followed through to the break-in at

the barricade surrounding the court. She squeezed her way through a crack in the wall. But it wasn't a break-in. She had been scanning the combative scenes on the walls when the court messenger found her.

A ray of light flashed through the crack, enveloping her. The light shone across every nook and cranny of the court premises. It drew the attention of all to watch this spectacle. The spy approached her.

"What do you search for among the debris?" he asked.

"I seek evidence to develop a story of events at the barricade."

She picked up some gravel and granite chips from the crumbling barricade.

"These chips pieced together and formed a model of the barricade." The spy showed with his hands.

The spy told Madika how officials went back and forth, taking the debris from the site to the museum.

"But why?" Madika asked

"Technocrats had been in the process of rebuilding the barricade. However, it seemed a herculean task. The prospects of reconstruction were diminishing. They thought the pieces of the barricade were better preserved at the tomb museum. They could piece the pieces together to form a model."

"Where can such a model be located?"

"The model has been taken to the museum. It was one of those inventions following the break-in at the barricade. Technocrats were enthusiastic about its infrastructure. It has stayed long within the confines of the derelict walls of the museum, to be considered something of a historical antique."

The spy was watchful of Madika. Her burning enquiries knew no calm. The spy allowed her to come in secret and take details of the combative scenes at Tila Lake. She noticed a river divided into two armies. Crocodiles in the river. There, she also noticed where a tomb was located. This made her recall the *bearer's* report of the river girl. The spy suspected her frequent visits and her scanning of the combative scenes on the walls of the court.

Madika was hopeful she would find hints about the river girl at the barricade. She thought of visiting the tomb museum, which was not far away from the barricade, to enhance her search. The building was one of the so many decayed structures. Its prison walls spoke of the many failed rehabilitation attempts to keep prying eyes out. The tomb museum received more frequent visits by fanatics in search of meanings for these objects.

Gravel and granite chips were scattered about as if to remind one of what befell the barricade before its transformation.

"It must have moved location through the years to be considered an antique," Madika said to the spy.

"It remains relevant as a reference point."

The tomb museum was housed in a derelict building, which brought to the fore the decay from yesteryear. Footpaths to the tomb could not be erased. It must have been engraved on the ground. Fanatics were often found lurking around the tomb. Others purposefully take a pilgrimage with questions on their minds—to get clues about the lives of the dead.

They constructed new meanings from previous expeditions, especially since the crocodiles walked away. These propagated beliefs on visits to the tombs of those who made history. They will uncover some truth. Because of the lack of provisions for such visits, the findings were suspicious. Leading to an uprising from various factions with counter-beliefs. The tomb served as a museum containing art designs of the war, sketches of battlegrounds, and the meeting of armies. Some of these were sketches as events unfolded at the barricade.

Some sketches described the path to the tombs. This was buried along with the finds, as anyone who unravels the *sketches* will understand the secrets behind the finds. The *sketches* unravel as Madika continues her journey. Madika, like others, had found her way there. Madika had approached. Lurking around—till she suspected some movements about the tomb.

A crocodile relic was found alongside others. On examination, the relics seemed to be the bird creature with a tail. These were preserved and kept under lock and key. It was believed that a guard kept watch over such finds in a building to prevent the reappearance of the creature. The building had become derelict, and the bird creature was all too soon forgotten.

A tap on these *sketches* would reveal the relationships and events in succession. This would surely alert the guard of an intruder. She knew of the *sketches* drawn on the ground from her past life. She remembered these faintly. However, Madika had frequent prompting of the *sketches*.

She wanted to bring to the surface that which was buried.

The relic gave some hints about the river girl since it formed sketches of the battleground. Madika learnt about the river girl in books. She twists like a river as fortune dictates. The melodies and tunes dictated the girl's dancing by the river. For the girl lived by the river and brought good fortunes. That stream the people went to for fertility. Some went to appease the river and avert war. The river girl's dancing was an offer of acceptance. The drums spoke to the river.

A second tap on the *sketch* would amplify the crocodile relic, such that it jumped out at her. She had realised the river girl. What clues she might have left behind following the invasion?

Out of the rumble, the portrait of the river girl emerged. She was thought to be dead. Some people must have thought of the contrary. The river girl was concealed beneath the relic made of stone. It was as though she had never escaped.

The conservationist had deemed the river girl a perfect resting place. Yamtarawala sought to depose the conservationist during his sojourn to Biu. Yet Yamtawarala's identity has been a cause of controversy.

Some argue his face was tattooed on the arms of the spies. The spies had also been secretly looking for the river girl. Thus, Yamtawarala evokes memories of the barricade, the court—and how it constitutes a workable relationship with the Biu people.

Men of Yamtarawala's court had emissaries as spies, but who were bound by oath as they were prone to betrayal. They were rewarded with enviable positions in the court. They worked in a closed alliance with the military arm. Their motto: *There is a spy in all of us.*

Court messengers handled the dissemination of everyday information. The spies moved insidiously among targets, exploiting relationships. To accurately account for losses and gains during wars. Or even modify such to guide the dissemination of information by messengers.

There were Yamtarawala's loyalists and others. Reporters could use these distinctions to sway the public from the actual issues at hand. For example, they described those in favour of dissolving the military arm of the court as saboteurs.

There was folklore in Yamtarawala up against Tila Lake. Some believed the hill from which he took a pose with the crocodile overshadowed Tila Lake. Others thought it overshadowed some river where he sought a maiden.

Some say it was around here that the barricade was constructed, and Yamtarawala could best trace the river he sought from here. He would give anything to gain such lands.

Enthusiastically, she proceeded from her enclosure. But with caution. By now she popped her head out, so you are in no doubt about her appearance. She had been forgotten about for a long time. It was believed she had flowed with the river into Tila Lake. You could tell she was not long out of the water. Her hair was constantly dripping with water. Even her entire body.

The river girl stepped out of her enclosure. Her steps awakened ghosts in the tomb. The objects scattered about, tracing sketches, arousing curiosity in the hearts of religionists. The relics had been in such a state waiting to be read; hence, they emerged like ghosts from the tomb. Such priceless artefacts were hidden from a public that groped in the dark.

The objects trailed sketches by which Madika identified their essence. Madika was still admiring this relic. But dropped the relic and started leaving the scene. Her footsteps led to some *sketches* on the walls. Madika unearthed the *sketches* that had travelled to the tomb. Its propagation. Through symbols embedded in various contexts, making beliefs. The *sketches* were formed by tracing the symbols on the objects. The objects frittered away with Madika's gaze.

Religionists followed the sketches trailed by the objects. The throng of people invaded the derelict tomb building to encounter modelled finds of a bird species previously swept under the carpet. They forced their way through the doors. Their stampede drowned the voices of ghosts awakening, causing reverberations. With these discoveries, their campaigns gained momentum as they took their protests to the *court gates*. This threatened the foundations of the court as the managers scampered off their seats.

They proceeded in Madika's direction. They did not know the essence of the *sketches*. The river girl had been reawakened. Madika started running, seeing the mob. She pulled the river girl out of the rumble so that two people were now running. The river girl's footpaths were the most slippery of paths, as the water kept dripping from her body. The water was building up again, such that she was causing a flood. There was none to stop her.

Water was slipping up through the walls. These reverberations alerted the guard, who came running. Madika had seen the old man at one entrance and had sneaked in through the other before he reached where she was. She was too fast for him. It was as though a ghost had emerged from the tomb. Such was her speed. The man had disappeared some 200 yards when she followed a sharp bend. It seemed she lost her assailant. But the old guard had noted her features. His eyes followed her everywhere she went.

She made away with the *sketches*. The old man could note her features and was bound to locate her at some point. Their paths would cross again because she had been there. He was the guard that would fight you at the scene of a crime, and his eyes followed you everywhere, as long as you made off with a material at the tomb site.

Exhausted, she stopped at a convenient point to rest. She wondered how the guard had noticed her almost immediately. She thought he must have noted her facial features through some technology. This bothered her even more. She felt now that some assailants must be on her trail. "*What do I do now?*" she asked. The thought of contacting the *bearer's associates* came to her mind, but she had lost the connection. She would need to do some consultations at the place she was dropped off to communicate with them. But she was far away from there. She also thought little of going to see the spy. Besides, what advice would he give her? He wasn't aware of her first adventure. She was unlikely to get anything progressive from him at the moment, except some advice on caution. She knew that wasn't what she needed most. She needed to cover her tracks, and the clock was ticking.

The guard walked off some distance away from the tomb to take some notes on the incident. These were instantly communicated to the men sitting on a court panel. They stared at each other in disbelief. "Who could have done this?" asked one of them.

The derelict building was crumbling down. It seemed like an earthquake. Who or what should be held responsible? Luckily, there was no loss of lives. Technocrats confirmed they hadn't studied the extent of such vibration in the past. Perhaps this would be a new area of research.

The stampede of ghosts followed the trails of the river girl. The river girl left vibration trails behind as she did at the barricade. "She has been here," they concluded. She has caused the crumbling down of the derelict building.

Technocrats from the secretariat came to the scene to investigate the cause of the vibrations of the buildings around the tomb. They took some debris from the collapsed building. The officials found crocodile symbols in objects. The objects were shared across government departments as a way of propagating beliefs. The objects trailed sketches of different sojourns. That was the essence of the disruption.

This propagation occurred by *sketches*. The *sketches* were symbolic of the paths of messengers and predictive of such fortunes that flowed with the river. The relic was passed along a chain of messengers. Passed through the hands of messengers seen bubbling on the surface of the river. But the *sketches* had been long forgotten since the children sketched in the sand. The river girl was at it again. It seemed the river girl was the last of such messengers.

This time, Madika had an accomplice. But the river girl was long gone. She had completely dissolved into Tila Lake.

Madika had picked up all these on her sojourn. Though sporadically, its meanings were waiting to be read. It sure must have some destination. Looking at the chase and her scramble for it. The invader mentality didn't inspire her. There was no case of theft. What we could recount was disruption and destruction, leading to the loss of valuables by an army of invaders.

Priests failed to explain the commotion caused by the *sketches*. They were taken aback. Fanatics, who once looked up to the priests, looked elsewhere as their gaze followed Madika.

The fanatics looked up to Madika for direction, as the priests had failed. They would have proceeded from the tomb like worshippers in an orderly procession. But there were no guidelines to follow. So many silent queries were made in the heart of the people. Things had spiralled out of control.

Detectives requested Madika for questioning. If for anything, as a witness. But what use would they make of such a witness? She might have triggered the events, but it had spiralled out of her control. The detectives were now on Madika's trail. The intruder had to answer for her crimes. They stopped by all those she may have been in contact with.

Headline: *Hoodlums vandalised the museum. The river girl, previously thought dead, emerged from the tomb. A woman stole artefact sketches from the tomb at midnight. Chief security is looking for a woman with familiar features bound to come his way. Trigger shock waves across the villages.*

They secretly sought the meaning of the *sketches*, as it triggered events in the past. Yet, they felt the river girl might have been behind the flood at the museum. Controversy would answer for controversy. Madika had been identified at the scene of social unrest. The trigger was the tap on the relic Madika had found. To awaken the objects at the tomb, the crocodiles walked from the river bank. The bird creature must be appeased since the crocodiles have left their habitat.

5

There were such rumours about Madika's unlawful romance with the spy who found her wandering. She considered these distractions. She needed some guidance on how to proceed. A path no one walked before. She struggled against such inclinations, as though fate would reward her and put her on the right path. It was therefore natural, given her dilemma, to drift to her comfort zones, where she found solace in Tila Lake's waters.

Madika's gaze concentrated on the reflections of Tila Lake's waters. The depths of the water—what came to its surface. You felt the breeze oozing out. Scenes of the past and present: Soothsayers approached Tila Lake with burning inquiries. The emergence of messengers that chose the *bearer*—a thing of political discourse. Paying obeisance to past *bearers* as people approached the *perimeter*. The crocodiles had retreated gradually into the lake. *Lovers* were soaked in this ambience. The bird creature must be doing something in the mound, as it wouldn't come out. It was *lovers'* hour.

The first scene had come and gone. Now the second—*bearers*, their torches, and the paths they followed. This scene was sketchy. We know the *bearer* performed rites on behalf of Biu indigenes. He was referred to as the *bearer* because of his eventful journey to Tila Lake on such occasions. But he usually came back alive from the journey.

These scenes ran through her mind. The torches as connecting paths. These are the paths that the *bearers* follow. The paths of the crocodiles. In the water, it seemed the torches were glued to the heads of the *bearers*. The *bearers* had completed their journeys satisfactorily. Some of them were now dead long ago. But for a *bearer* who began his journey, the torch led the way to touch on points toward Tila Lake. The *bearers* were those foretold to carry out the rituals at Tila Lake. Some would rather refer to them as *fore-bearers*. Their torches paved the paths they followed. The rituals were to renew the potency of the water as a recourse for control. Where the past and present scenes were viewed—only from here could practices be reviewed. By towing the paths of his *fore-bearers*, the *bearer* navigated his path.

Each glimpse of Tila Lake brought different scenes—in the rotating fashion of the past and present. Like being in a living museum with revolving doors reflecting. You come to immerse yourself in its splendour. A museum is not just for a collection of artefacts. But it gives you an experience that is transferable to everyone alike. Madika had been in such a museum. Her experience filtered to others.

Tila Lake contained the participation of everyone—their convergence and divergence points. The water struggled to go its way. But it was trapped by the battling of the crocodiles. Such is Tila Lake. The crocodiles in the glistening water were a disguise for the tourists. The tourists examined a collection of events. And for *lovers* who came in their droves. From them, the radiation emanated in ripples.

Here, she may have encountered the *bearer's* associates. Madika was within reach of the *bearer's associates*. But the associates formed a closed group, which she was trying to get into. It seemed they guarded the secrets of Tila Lake.

They wouldn't let such things out easily the way the spy had about the river girl.

They might send for Madika after some consideration. What would that be? Madika was now within touching distance of their floating bodies. They knew of Madika's sojourn, as she became transparent the floating bodies eventually met.

Madika feared for her life. However, she felt as though she was being carried in safe hands. It was as though she would be deposited on the banks of Tila Lake. But she had navigated the remotest paths of Tila Lake.

The *bearer's associates* led Madika through the entry points of Tila Lake. She swarmed her way through all the hurdles. Learning the ropes. She saw the connecting paths of the *bearer*. Despite having a different mission, she could easily be classified as a *bearer*. She was the one to expose buried secrets long forgotten. But first, she had to go through the *process of finds*. This she found intriguing and wouldn't leave the *seabed*. But she jerked up at once. Then she remembered she had been floating. She did sense communication links to the bird creature, though that was a distant dream.

Madika had been discovered too early, hence the need for hibernation. She lived in the wild. This was acceptable to her, having undergone some training. She would submit to one official, who would provide some hints on the *bearer's* journey. Madika would follow such hints, having learnt such codes of communication from the spy.

She had been forced to investigate the *bearers'* path. And even the crocodiles in Tila Lake. She had become a confidant of the *bearer*. She knew of the depths of the lake. What she never imagined would come true in such a manner. She would require some respite when she visits again, by which time she must have been old. But the paths never grew old. These had always been relevant and beyond manipulation by the *council of finds*. At least they now found something, if not her. But the *bearer's* associates wouldn't reveal the circumstances in which she was found.

Suddenly Madika realised the *bearer's* associates were gone. She was left alone. Her mind flashed to the spy. She might have wished to see him again and ask further questions. Perhaps tell him of her plight. But this was a memory she would rather relish alone. It gave her a sense of purpose. If she were to reveal it to the winds, it would wither away, and they might soon start looking for her. She felt safe as long as this experience stayed with her. She could walk unnoticed around the scene where it all started. Her facial features had been modified through many days of exploration in the waters. Her encounters had shaped her vision.

She knew how the river girl escaped from being captured at the barricade. During her sojourn, she encountered a force that brought her close to Tila Lake's perimeter. She noticed the *perimeter* retreated, only to gather more strength on its return. It retreated to a point where the bird creature appeared. If it appeared at such an instance, it could grant the seeker's wishes of the lake, as a mode of communication was open. In all other instances, the *perimeter* was a barrier. This could be for several reasons, which the creature elaborated on. The *bearer* had sought to approach the lake at such a time when the *perimeter* barred him from approaching further.

She sought the mechanisms that could weaken the *perimeter* when the bird creature appeared. It seemed the power of the creature lay on the *perimeter*. That power repelled people from coming closer.

The spy appeared again to Madika. This time he was on her trail, as he suspected of her disappearance.

He had been waiting for her all day. She walked into his arms as if to give him a hug. But he was steady as a rock. *Did she also feel the same?* Her eyes transfixed on him to complete the process of exploration. Their minds now joined as one. A powerful force waiting to explode.

"I have been sitting here all day. Where have you been?" She was trying to recollect her thoughts.

"I must have been caught up in my little world. I have been searching for you since the last time. Now you are at your favourite spot."

"Well, my thoughts about you have changed in the last few days. I think you will join me soon at my favourite spot. I still seek the relevance of the *perimeter*."

"*The mysterious thing about Tila Lake is its formation. It seemed I found my way out of the courts to observe the activities there. Then I felt like escaping,*" said the spy.

This reminded him of one of his glimpses at Tila Lake during a court recess. Such tales one may learn from those who had been to Tila Lake. Those who wanted freedom had found it— freedom from their past. They now observe their past like those who regard the patterns formed by the swarms of crocodiles. They were engrossed because they had seen striking details of their past. It only led to being more curious—they had become *lovers* at Tila Lake. Partners' hands in gloves were seen along the lake's *perimeter*.

"Whoever told you about this lake?" Madika asked the spy.

The spy had become familiar to her as they had similar quests.

"I was part of an expedition when we crossed the lake's path. And on a path to self-discovery. We searched for freshly swept snails as we moved near. The emerging waves repelled us further, realising we were at Tila Lake's *perimeter*. Those at the front line of the expedition retreated until the message was passed to me. We were a chain of messengers."

"Did you get to see the snails you were looking for?"

"Those who got to the snails were amused and started tracing where the line emerged from, taking them to a hole of water where cries were heard. It seemed the water had swept up the snails."

"How far was the line traced to the water?"

"The holes formed a pattern around the water body. It was at an equal distance from each point of reference. It spread in concentric circles, as one could note the history of other circles. They knew they were within the sight of a water body. It was unexpected. We reported the incident when we got back."

"How were the holes formed and for what purpose?"

"The snails bore holes with sharp protruding tubes like spears. The holes formed tunnels of water as the *bearers* approached. Thus, they performed the rites."

"Did it feel dangerous crossing its path?"

"Not really. It only made you even more curious. Just a feeling that there is more than meets the eye."

"They must know of a way of its preservation. Maybe that's why they wouldn't have people go there. Did you expect what was in the lake?"

"I suspect the water sourced from the lake was kept in jars of water. Such objects were a resource to control Tila Lake. When the water was fetched, the *perimeter* was still and no longer subject to the crocodile's instructions."

"I never came across any documents regarding its preservation. Although it is possible, such was discussed behind closed doors. The crocodiles were the occupants of the lake."

"Hmm. There is longevity in secrecy."

"Will there be longevity in the secrets I told you?"

"You talked of preservation. I have started some preservation projects already. I have strewn straws woven into shapes. I picked such from the ground just like you wanted to pick the snails."

"Interesting. What would you do with the snails if you could pick them?"

"Create a habitat for them, so that they are not found, where you can pick them."

"But you know we could not pick them. They were within the *perimeter*."

"Do you suspect the snails may know something about the *perimeter*?"

"I wouldn't know. The pattern of holes around the water body formed the *perimeter*."

"That means there are secrets about the crocodile unknown to the people. I must have been suspecting this longer than I imagined?"

"How do you mean?"

Now she felt compelled to tell of her experience in the hands of the bearer's associates. The many visions at the depths of the water. The court messenger also appeared to be one who could be trusted. She might have longed to share these memories with him. She emerged from the waters and was extremely afraid of seeing the crocodiles rush back to the lake. Where had they all gone initially? But she hesitated and instead gave him an optimistic look.

"There could be some finds worthy of exploration in the lake. I suspect that brings about its mysteriousness. Some comprehend the exploratory nature of these finds, while others link them to the crocodiles' disappearance." She concluded.

Not everyone can come to such a conclusion, as their experiences on Tila Lake differ.

She also recalled that the *bearers* had vanished from the scene as soon as she emerged, leaving her in a state of confusion.

Having sensed the risk of her continued presence, she went into hiding. She feared the government officials might express some suspicion and trace all her contacts. Had they seen her talking with the spy? It looked unlikely, but the possibility hung in the balance.

Meanwhile, the *bearer's associates* were doing all they could to erase all traces of their contact with Madika. This included the points of meeting and departure. Her sojourn into the waters was to conceal all such traces. The *bearer's associates* could divert all connecting points; linking the paths away from the crocodiles such that she didn't meet them. As soon as she concluded her sojourn, the crocodiles came rushing. Emerging, she met the spy. This meeting was unknown to the *bearer's associates*, but she quickly realised her sojourn. And was hurrying away.

"I have to go now," she said just as before."

"I recall that you may have to go, eventually."

"Our paths will cross again."

She was away before the next reply came. This left the spy thinking about himself again. That was his fate—such events he got entangled with. He had accepted such fate, knowing that he would always come out victorious on the other side. A mission accomplished. What mission was unclear to him now? He smiled and walked away.

Looking at the *sketches*, Madika wondered why she left off with it. But it was the first thing that caught her eye. She looked at it again, then started taking strides in admiration of this new gift. The strides led her to unknown places she relished as familiar. She kept dragging on against her wish, but couldn't fathom any known obstacle. She seemed to have forgotten about her predicament. Her resolve led her to follow the paths until visible footprints were leading the way.

Her sojourn took her through various landmarks on the journey. She arrived at the *perimeter* unannounced and with little protocol. She looked around to see if anyone was coming. But no, she was alone. The *perimeter* caved in, allowing her to see the length and breadth of the lake. She recalled where she had exited the last time. But could not see the entry point. She admired the patterns formed by the array of crocodiles, wondering what would disrupt it. She had been to Tila Lake and became a *lover*. She stood out from the other *lovers*. Her burning enquiries knew no calm. A flame dancing in the waters.

Her company of *lovers* had deserted her now. She was alone and wanted company. She felt like rushing into the court messenger's embrace. She could explain his feelings. He must have been to Tila Lake—or around here. The lake's water was getting brighter as she gazed across its surface. Other patterns were visible, like the writings of a hand. The patterns spanned centuries.

Madika recalled her sojourn to Tila Lake— accompanied by the *bearer's* associates. When she was deserted, she recalled her conversations with the messenger. How he felt the same. The signs were clear: The court messenger should also involve in this quest. That's why they were having similar feelings. It seems this was known to the *bearer's* associates, too. But they had been waiting for the time for all to be revealed. The messenger was neck-deep in the protocols in the courts. He needed to raise his head above the waters to have some breath of fresh air. His soul mate, bound to him by fate—Madika—was good at swimming underneath the water looking for some finds. She would emerge again with burning enquiries, like a flame dancing in the waters.

She might seem even stranger to the messenger. As he moved closer to his routines, he showed more dedication, even commitment, to the senior members at the bar. His vision was clearer now. He realised Madika must be at odds with this clique. He was the mediator between the two, as both sides required his attention. He must now give up the courts to be fully embraced with Madika. The court messenger would improvise on the laws— to permit such association, but he had to climb up the ranks. By which time he might be more interested in the collection of levies.

She might go to the *bearer's* associates through the same mode of communication to tell them of her plight. In an instant, she was connected to them. And could see their faces in the reflections as though they had not once departed. In a confused state, she tried to make out their faces. But they called her from beneath the waters as if to drag her in. She recalled again how she was dragged here. Now she was alert and ready for their instructions.

"You need to present the sketches to an interpreter to proceed on your journey. He knows that you have been here. It is time now."

They disappeared in the same instant, leaving her more confused now. But the only access she had to the courts was through the messenger. What would he think of her? He must also have heard of the theft. Would she resolve it all simultaneously? The questions kept running through her mind. But she later felt there must be a connection between the two events. She expected some magic, but couldn't tell how it was going to work.

The search team went about their daily chores, sniffing out information from every nook and cranny—like dogs. They had been set loose. Everyone feared their houses might be checked for every trace of Madika. Shock waves sent shivers down the spine of the villagers as the river girl's reappearance was distressing. Immediately, there was a census. The people formed groups.

The counting began with the beating of drums. This forced out some confessions. The beats sounded familiar and placated some. Then they were withdrawn into shelters for some respite. Meanwhile, some volunteered to join the search, committing themselves and others. Their wishes were granted, as time was of the essence.

Madika prowled around in the shadows, leaning behind trees, and counting till she got to a safe abode. The *bearer's associates* had given her directions. She left for a long time, exiled away from everyone else. The *bearer's associates* had turned their backs, telling her not to look back until she found an interpreter.

As she held onto the *sketches*, she felt the interpreter draw close. The interpreter read the *sketches* on her palm and told her how far she had come. The *sketches* propelled her onward. *The sketches revealed the pathway of the codes. The rhythms of the drums mixed with Tila Lake waters.* Such resonance was required to allow Madika a hitch-free journey. The man symbolised other creatures she must have met beneath the water. So, she had put all her experiences to use.

She came to the full realisation of the prompting of the *sketches*. *The interpreter as messenger. To dictate the pathways of sketches. The sketches drawn by the children travelled to the walls of the tomb.* The interpreter narrated how she would proceed on her journey and who she should meet. This gave her some assurance to pursue her mission further until she got to the wild. Seeing the same number of trees, she met, gathered again, as if to welcome her. Like spears encircling an enemy. She screamed in horror. As she was led to her abode and promised some rest. She was cut from everyone, even the events that led her to the wild.

PART
TWO

6

Walking back home now with reminiscences of past events. Children dashed across the streets without fear of cattle that came thumping along. When the latter saw them, they simply heaved their horns to give the children more space to play. When the children saw corps members who were non-indigenes, they shouted "*kopi kopi*" and ran into hiding. They imitated a headteacher who called a corps member. That call was to alert you they had been lurking around, waiting for the opportune moment.

Biu indigenes were happy to see us. The thrill was on their faces as they ran. Was it our uniforms that enticed them? Or because they saw us coming from *makaranta*? Some of the Biu indigenes we taught were familiar to us. The girls behind their hijabs—and the boys who went to Islamic school after school hours. What would they have thought of the *Almajiris* prowling the streets for food? The doctrine of *Almajiri* was important to them in these parts. This they have heard all their lives.

It was the difference in looks between Southerners and Northerners—and their perceptions. The indigenes were used to different people coming and going. Perhaps they thought we were tourists. We were. We saw the culture here. They must have heard tales of those who came here from the South.

They must have felt we had come from afar to make some contribution to the community. Like the missionaries who came to Garkida.

People on the sidewalks awaited a greeting. I walked past them, greeting, *"sannu ku."* With each greeting, you got closer to the people. They lived communally. Home is the place of rest from their activities. Whether you were back from school, the market, or the farm.

Home is cool—when not sunny. I had been in the companionship of a table, chair, and mattress. Roundabout were the four bare walls staring at me just as I did the same.

I was sure I heard the door open. Then I remembered I did not close it earlier. Samuel, a prudent Agric economist who often talked about relating theory to practice, had arrived. I heard him asking what made Benue State—the food basket of the nation. "How many baskets of food come from there?" He asked. Samuel must have just walked through the adjacent door. He wasn't disposed to talking. But came out of his room almost immediately to check the growth of his crops. There he was, almost completely hidden in the crops he planted some months ago. He made it a point of duty to water these crops every morning. And I assisted him with this.

He was so engrossed in his work that he hardly noticed my presence. He looked up at each stalk, searching for worms. Some leaves were eaten by insects. Disappointed, he dashed back in a flash, brought out a medicinal powder, and started spraying the leaves indiscriminately. Subsequently, he closely bent to each one and almost kissed one. He stayed long in wishful thinking, hoping his medicine would work this time.

Just then, I called out to Samuel twice. He wouldn't respond. The leaves' fragrance intoxicated him. He seemed to dream of a bountiful harvest.

"Soon they will queue for my vegetables," he

declared at once. He emerged victorious from his expedition. With a tinge of satisfaction on his face, he said, "I can't believe how fast they have grown. I can now relate theory to practice. It differs from being in a classroom."

The leaves had been some sort of excitement to us—seeing how fast they had grown. Soon they would grow into trees. It was pleasurable to see Miringa soil yield increase. The crops had taken over the entire space. You had to shove them to the side to pass.

I felt for Samuel. Sometimes it could get lonely here. And the leaves were the only objects of admiration.

After the market day, the people returned to their normal routines. Mr Yaya was seen going to *makaranta*. He held his books in hand and walked fast to get to the assembly line just in time. His students were already assembled. *Makaranta*, as they saw it, differed from the Islamic school the students went to—after *makaranta*. *Makaranta* was the convention for learning; the Islamic school was everyday learning. In the eyes of such convention were the corps members seen— those that flood the streets in trickles, but got noticed by everyone alike. "He is going to *makaranta*," says one. The other watched with some queer curiosity. Yet their kids also attended *makaranta*—though absentmindedly. *Makaranta* formed an attachment to some classes of people, and rhetoric to others. Though they attended *makaranta* before going to the Islamic school, the latter was far more important to them.

Makaranta contrasted with the Islamic school in several ways. Foremost was the lifestyle. The second was perception. From first and second: Perceptions were formed from lifestyles. Graduates from an Islamic school were held in high esteem. The traditional system here was of the emirate. Positions in this hierarchy are thus assigned. The *Almajiri* might have looked up to this. Suffer now, enjoy later.

We just left *makaranta*. Coming along the major road, we walked until we were at the market. We had passed the burning, yet we could smell the incense coming from it. A place of worship. Places of worship were in proximity to marketplaces and homes. Was the incense meant to make appeasement for the *bearer's* safe return? The rites were being performed again for a normal resumption of market activities. For us, it was time again to take a break from *makaranta* duties.

You could take a curious look at daily events at the Miringa market from one of these tea shop compartments. You were likely partly concealed by persons sighted about you. You were in a carriage. A mobile tea shop that stopped momentarily—now permanently. When you stopped by, the carriage stopped; you were allowed entry by the opening on either side.

"*Sannu ku*," greeted the entrant.

And those in the carriage replied, "*sannu da zuwa*." You were welcomed from the side to which you gained entry. It was clear why the carriage stopped, and there was no need to ask. You settled down to business.

"*Bani kunu da kosai mana*," you requested breakfast. As you were eating, you perceived the *Almajiris* waiting by the side of the carriage. They could not come in grand style and appreciate the carriage as you just had. Their eyes were fixed on the measure of pap and baked beans that the seller dished out to you. From this point, you could see various trading units: cigarettes and hot drinks sold here. Curtains were drawn apart to display the items in the units. Metal-making shops and many artworks were also on display. Samuel and Co. were about here. They were taking a break from *makaranta* duties.

Samuel developed a weird interest in theatre. I would never have imagined he'd go to the playhouse to watch characters come up on stage and perform. He had even watched them wear their costumes and outfits and said one dressed like his grandfather. He must have taken after the old man then. But the old tricks differed from those he always wanted to watch. He seemed only interested in the actors and actresses following a script. After which, they could laugh out of the sight of the audience. He would usually have preferred comical characters. His preference was likely because of his hectic routine.

Samuel had identified some of the regular performers and had been speaking to them. Unknown to me, they were discussing forming their band. The idea was to have a mobile playhouse where their audience was everywhere they went. Samuel would start on a serious note, then clowns would take over. One particular script involved the bird creature and the officer. One of them foolishly thought he could invite the bird creature for interrogation.

"Why can't that be?" he countered.

"Because it can't be," was the reply.

Certain replies could only quieten the clowns. They mastered their art, to the amazement of all and sundry. Some even gave them tips for their efforts. Something Samuel frowned at. The clowns had taken over the performance—even the practices of the playhouse. Samuel was the only patron to hold the group accountable. And, ironically, for representation.

The clowns were about to meet and perform again. At Samuel's displeasure, they began disturbing the peace in pubs and bars. But it all started and ended in music and dancing. They could take care of themselves, after all. Some of them were graduates like Samuel, whose aim was to reach out to the community through the arts. Samuel was an economist, so his role was an accountant.

"Our students are something else," Samuel commented as he sipped a hot drink. He was in one carriage about here. "Some of them spy on us while we are having our performances. Even when we didn't intend to amuse the audience, we found them laughing."

"What was funny? Were they secretly wishing to be actors and actresses?" the clowns asked.

"I wouldn't know. I know little about sourcing talents here."

"Do you think they would be of any help?"

"They would make young, vibrant actors and actresses. Some could be excellent performers in comic roles... I once heard such melodious beats from a youthful drummer. You could communicate with the sounds from a distance. He must have been drumming since he was a youth. He drew his audience nigh from the crowd."

7

In Miringa, there was pride in racing with motorcycles. You called an *achaba* when you intended one to stop, and it conveyed you to your destination. On arrival, you said, "*nan.*" You also saw tricycles—someone was riding through the town with loud music. Sometimes he'd be speeding on rough terrain. You'd fear he'd have an accident, but he emerged victorious.

In the afternoon, you saw the Fulani in their clothing decorated with beads going about their business. They almost went unnoticed by the Bura. Their pilgrimage from sunrise to sunset marked a turn of events. Soon after their passage, you might decide to buy some food from a hawker. Or decide to close for the day. As you went home, you said a greeting to virtually everyone that came your way. Some may be familiar to you; others you might have seen at other times while walking the same paths.

The Fulani lined the streets in colours that shone one after the other. It was easy to forget that you just saw one till another came along. Walking in footsteps almost unheard, they trailed familiar footpaths till they vanished from sight.

The songs and sounds were familiar to us as we danced to their rhythms. The songs occasioned events when the strings were plucked. There was such vibration everywhere. That faint sound picked up suddenly and rhythmically. We sat across tables, waiting to gulp down some beer. The excitement continued, with music jostling between the talking. Yet you might decipher what was being said across tables.

The girls came in hawking meat pepper soup. Then we ordered more beer. After the musical notes died, memories were vivid. "Where did these girls come from?" Someone asked casually.

Then, a man staggered in, speaking volubly yet with some discretion. It appeared as though he was philosophising. He reeled out; he made out his tale: "*They looked at a girl from behind. They spoke ill of her, though she was beautiful. They objected to her way of life.*" The man felt ashamed now that he was drawing attention to himself.

Drunken scenes were not rampant. But some were remarkable. The men sitting at the table thought of him as a philosopher. How was it he was philosophising in a drunken state? But he reserved the right to a performance. Weren't the people nodding to the drumming? And dancing imperceptibly, even in their drunken states? But they wouldn't agree they were drunk. It was this man who was drunk. He put on performances that weren't anticipated.

"*No, I must continue.*" The philosopher summoned his courage. He smirked as if to start his tale again from the beginning or where he stopped. It seemed the girl in question was mistaken for someone else. But her detractors were those well known to her. What went around came to stay. Here with her. It was obvious she was just being picked on for mischief.

The men sat in a half-circle. Spoke one to another, then turned to the man.

"Where is this girl from?" they asked the philosopher.

He ignored the question and turned to his performance as if to continue with it. But before then, he ordered a bowl of *burukutu*. This drink was made from guinea corn after fermentation. It tasted good. Rich in colour with good flavour. Sometimes it was the drink we chose for the occasion in the evenings. It could make you go pee a few times. With such satisfaction, you were back to join the discussion.

He continued now with a pitiful demeanour: "*Oh the weevils from her side. I hope they didn't see it. Probably they were carried away in mischief.*" Now another weevil, then it was obvious. The philosopher stopped for a while.

Ibrahim walked in like a ghost that had come at will, though without many ghoulish tendencies. But with a seemingly friendly demeanour. His feet were bitten by rain and sun. His mouth was cracked, yet gave out a wide smile. He usually knew almost everyone in such social settings. And might not throw in much courtesy before joining the fray. Ibrahim was identified as Bura. He had friends from all social classes. He could have been the one being spoken about. Or flattered. Directing all the faces in his direction as he walked in. Just as the girl in question walked in from the other direction.

What would one make of such beauty? The strings of beads danced about her waist, her eyelashes and her eyebrows. Her hair was plaited, and she was courteous. Suddenly, the philosopher called out,

"Hanatu!" out of his drunkenness. She swiftly attended him.

"Did I call you?" he asked.

"You did," the girl replied.

"*Sannu.*"

"*Ina wuni lafiya,*" she replied again.

"I was thinking about another *burukutu* but realised I still had some here."

"It's OK. You can make your request when appropriate." She went, then turned back.

"Do you know him?" she asked, pointing in the direction Ibrahim had come from.

"Why would you ask if I know him? Are you referring to him?" He looked in Ibrahim's direction.

"I just wasn't expecting I would see him here again… I was at home one day tending the garden when two men walked into my compound asking for, Mr Ibrahim. They came on a motorcycle…" She stopped. "He wore the same look as the first time. He looks like an inspector."

"In that case, he must have come around unnoticed at other times. He might as well have just come for a drink, you never know."

"It has not been long since I started selling *burukutu* here…Well, he must have been here at other times."

"Ibrahim is not unfamiliar with these parts. He is well known in most parts of Biu and Miringa. He has connections with many people. Old, young, rich, and poor. *It is no coincidence we are talking about him now*." He smirked. "Interestingly, Ibrahim sees himself as Babur-Bura. He connects with both sides. A mediator between the two. He spoke a lot about Na'Allah's loyalty to the late emir. When we first met, he said he would subscribe to such loyalty. Only he loves to travel. I don't think he would maintain such a routine as Na'Allah's."

"Who is Na'Allah?" she asked.

"The Emir's bodyguard. It seems Ibrahim was in the military. That is the reason Na'Allah's fate particularly interested him. He had perspectives on Na'Allah's good sense of security. He wouldn't say if Na'Allah had a military mindset. But he was thrilled by his act of bravery. The tale of Na'Allah has been passed on through generations."

"I remember Ibrahim would salute the officers at the barracks as though he were in military service. *An old soldier never dies*."

You found such a secure and peaceful atmosphere at the barracks in Biu. Never mind the roadblocks on your way coming in. But once in, you found peace and tranquillity. Once you moved away from the quarters, you arrived at a market scene while moving from stall to stall.

Ibrahim must have wished he was still in military service. Just as he wished for Na'Allah. If wishes were horses… Everyone wished so for Na'Allah. Whatever happened to Na'Allah. I learnt he had a monstrous appearance and helped ward off enemies.

What happened to the Emir's bodyguard?

I passed through the hallway, which would echo by an attempt to feel them or by their sights. I looked straight ahead. Right in front was the *dogari*. They sat on the veranda in flowing gowns. Fixed on any visitor who came to the palace. You could see them from a distance. A first barrier to cross. They were a dedicated crop that beat around in still-like motions until the visitor had passed. Ceremonial, but dedicated. They had a boring gaze. Once you crossed that line, you almost forgot about it.

Peacocks were about, walking at varying angles till they gave way. Now the Emir was in sight. The Emir was in his gracious Babur-Bura attire, seated at a table. It was Sallah day. Dishes were served: *Janguli* (a mixture of groundnut, beans, guinea corn, and bambara nut), *nduva mthli* (food prepared from guinea corn), *buraku* (a traditional soup made from okro, beans, garden egg), and *thalalang* (traditional potash). Drummers at Hawul, dancing and singing his praises. All these to the delight of dignitaries and those present— the 27 district heads were at the palace.

The chief Imam gave the opening prayers, and each district head wore a *barmuzu* (a large flowing gown) with a spear in hand, riding on a horse with his representatives in front of them to pave the way. On getting to the Emir, they raised their spears three times, sticking them to the ground. After paying homage to the Emir, they went to their various lodges to prepare for the Sallah feast at the palace the following day.

The drummers had been producing different beats. They were a famous group of drummers in Biu that performed with Bukar Kpchi, who is famous in Hawul for *bonsue* dancing and drumming. I knew they were going to give those playing the *tibilau* some good backup tunes:

Kuthli Ali Lubarrahi Kuthli Ali Lar
Rikuthlhda Kuthli Ali Lubarrahi Ramta.

The Emir has travelled eastwards to Biu Kuthlga. To those in the West, the Emir has died.

Perched about the Emir were emissaries who

brought messages back and forth. To prepare for some august visitor who had come from afar, and left shoes behind with the *dogari*. The visitor approached Na'Allah.

Na'Allah was the Emir's prime *dogari*. It was said of Na'Allah. His tour from Azare (Hawul) to Sabon Kasuwa, Yirmirshika, Aga Bura, Barki Sakwa, Marama, Kidang, Durkwa, and then Kwaya Bura. Each giant stride covered each named location. And with beats as of Bukar kpchi.

The beating of the drums hastened his strides. Na'Allah met the Emir at Hawul, where he left off. His rounds were routine, which carried the Emir's presence. Such was his loyalty. When the Emir died, the sounds from the beating drums stopped, and Na'Allah's steps retracted. Na'Allah died.

Someone with a cigarette in hand peeped through the smoke-stained curtain. Taking his attention from the tête-à-tête. Anything to pass the time would do. The night was gradually creeping in.

"That girl can dance all night. She has danced again. I think the men are now trooping in," the philosopher was heard saying. The philosopher thought of the weevils on her waist as beads flipping up and down, catching the attention of men.

At night, we moved as shadows lodged in corners. The men drank all night while narrating events from the past. Sometimes the women drank too. Among men, those who drank were comparatively few. And it seemed most of these took place behind closed doors. The scenery was like any other. The music jostled among the talking. People were gathered in patches for merrymaking as the market moved at a slower pace. Livestock was not in sight.

Night brought cover on settled dust. Should we wait till it was day again? Wouldn't the people then be engaged in buying and selling? Na'Allah might appear in ghoulish form and walk the streets again.

"Where did this man get such philosophy?" they wondered. He was full of hope, yet unseen.

Adjusting his spectacles, the philosopher said, "Indeed, without looking too far, you can see a different side to life."

You can, during festivities, where quotes, memories, and personalities were evoked. Each of these provokes events with renewed significance. But this was not one such festive occurrence. We were weary of the subject and laid matters to rest rapidly.

Such was the nature of gossip in these parts. It seemed the philosopher knew that from the beginning of the conversation.

8

The beating of the drums continued. Na'Allah had awoken. Na'Allah sensed he had a task yet to be completed. Madika was to be presented to speak at the public square. She had to say what she knew about the disruption at the tomb museum.

Na'Allah had a sense of Madika's features and was prying about for her in calculated guesses. Madika was still fleeing the scene of disruption at the tomb. Word spread that Madika had the keys to fixing the barricade. Na'Allah was on her trail as other ghosts had done before. He had ears as big as a wolf. And had picked up such signals from her trail. To find her in isolation among the trees of horror, as she once knew. Recalling this event, she attempted to flee again but was grabbed by the hand. Someone unknown, with ghostly features, emerged from the shadows. But he was familiar to her.

Na'Allah had found her and brought her to the palace. She was awoken by his giant footsteps. He stopped hearing her panting. Took her by the arm and led her into the palace. She was ordered to the public square with guards on either side. To her left, those with the crocodile symbol on their uniforms, to her right, those without. Those at the public square were also divided along those lines.

Na'Allah was dragging her to the court gates, but the throng of people prevented him. The religionists carried placards with signs: restore our place of worship, Madika the invader. Others advocated for a fair trial.

She learnt in history books about those who faced a similar predicament. They were accused of inciting the public to violence and disrupting the peace. Interestingly, the consequences of fanaticism were also laid in their footsteps. Armed men seized them and forcefully put them into a building while they protested their arrests.

"You can't drag me like that," she protested her arrest. An officer showed her a warrant for her arrest.

"I will give you a chance to speak at the public square," the officer replied.

Madika sat unconscious as one hypnotised.

"You must give your evidence before the court." They kept dragging her.

They wanted a statement on what she knew about the events in the tomb, since they proved she had triggered the reverberations. Until now, no one understood the *sketches* or in what manner they might have triggered the reverberations. References to the *sketches* were long forgotten. They couldn't understand how the sketches of the children in the sand could relate to the reverberations. How did it evoke memories in Madika and no one else?

It seemed suspicious. It was as though she was concealing something. To be fair to her, some persons knew the reverberations would awaken the mass of the crocodile relics which had risen to the surface at the tomb. They had concluded the investigation on such a report, but kept it secret. They imagined Madika's sojourn in that direction.

What would wake the dead? Or make objects trail sketches and cause reverberations? They heard the bird creature speak—whose specimens they assumed were being cultured in the tomb? The children then could draw sketches that could cause the reverberations.

Madika was in a state of amnesia from the many shocks she had. She might not even have felt the weight of shackles on her legs if she had one on. Her entire body was numb. She required medical attention. She could hardly answer the questions before her. The search team had finally found her, but there was no motivation for her arrest. She had been relieved of the *sketches* by the interpreter. Her quest was suspended. The interpreter had disappeared into thin air just as he came. She answered questions via signs, and it was apparent she didn't recall a single word spoken to her.

Once she was revived, she recalled the scenes at Tila Lake. Her meeting with the *bearer's associates*. Her burning enquires—a flame dancing all around the waters. She launched for the lake again. This time, events would lead her to personal contact with the bird creature. This would elaborate further on her mission. Again, she relapsed into numbness.

The beating of the drums continued. This time to awaken her consciousness. Those who waited until this hour were jeering at her. Their efforts to join the search team were not in vain after all. She was twitching, showing different sides, like the crocodile. The jeering continued, but this time she went into the waters again. Her perspiration was profuse; the water gliding out from her body.

"Have we come to watch her perform magic here?" someone asked.

Madika had learnt the art of magic. The *sketches* brought out such tremendous energy. It allowed her to perform some conjuration, as she recalled where she had been. And the paths she followed. This was the motivation for her excitement.

Madika was joined by others arriving from the markets. They placed their empty baskets on the floor and started chanting, seeing Madika on display. They had little creative energy themselves, having spent all at the market. Otherwise, they would have formed groups of partners in a love like fashion. They could tell the performance was one which called for solidarity during trials. Even the search team and members of the national squad were taken aback, forgetting the obligation of the moment. The crocodile in their uniforms proceeded from their enclosures with smiley faces.

The court messenger was at the scene of Madika's display but thought little of it till he was at his desk. Then he remembered the subject of many years of investigation. *The sketches revealed the pathways of the codes. The rhythms of the drums mixed with Tila Lake's waters.* Madika had also come to such a realisation. The writings on the surface of Tila Lake must have been useful in such conjuration. It was the motivation for Madika's excitement. Such writings predate the formulation of statutes. This might have interested the court messenger.

The time and use of such conjuration had been spelt out to those who had shown sufficient dedication to the rites. Such was also the time of explosive economic boom in market activities. The court messenger recalled times of innovation at the courts and attributed the effects to the same cause. It seemed Madika was on the verge of fulfilment.

At the gathering, the atmosphere was charged enough to assume that there were many more people, like Madika. These were not on the run but, involved in the circulation of information that led to the gathering. They enquired about the search for Madika when she escaped the chase given by the guard. But the search was not about Madika. They had been on her trail ever since, watched her every move and speculated. But one thing was certain—she had caused disruptions just like the bird creature. It seemed she revealed the creature.

She might have discovered the weakest link of her assailants—that derelict building—far from everyone else. It seemed forbidden to go there, as its paths led to nowhere. Until the old guard emerged from its enclosure to question who dared to come near. The tombs here were mostly silent. However, it had seemed one of the dead gave the chase. Madika had drawn *sketches* from the wall, causing reverberations. Did they suspect Madika had found something being sought? The reverberations in the walls knocked off objects in the museum from their positions. The startled old man looked in Madika's direction as she began running. He had been performing some conjuration in the tomb museum—of all dead beings. He secretly investigated specimens of the creature to determine the authenticity of the *bearer's* report. Though Madika was unaware of this, she brought his quest alive, bringing his search to a close.

Madika had been on many journeys and only

recalled them faintly. She needed to eat some food, as she had been without some for days.

"Will you tell us what motivated you to visit the sacred tomb?" they asked her.

She was gesticulating with her hands, as if eager to answer and only requiring an interpreter. It was uncertain who that could be. *When did she resort to communication via signs? A once vocal personality whose protests went beyond the streets to every nook and cranny. Something terrible has happened to her. Has she got instant punishment from the gods? Do we still need to interrogate her further or trace her path?*

By now, they gathered to watch what spectacle Madika had come. The children spurred her to go on further exploits—not even minding that she sat on the floor eating with ten fingers. She had become the central character in stories told to them—both heard and read. In the end, she predicted her fate. She had been in vigorous pursuit of knowledge of everything around her, but now she had come here. It was clear her journey had ended.

9

Following the disruption at the tomb, the model of the barricade was recovered. A haggard, old man was excited by this development. He was on the lookout for news regarding the disruption at the tomb. He drew parallels between this event and the invasion at the barricade.

On examination, the haggard, old man made out the holes in the model. Being an engineer, he attempted to postulate the locations of holes that needed fixing to prevent water flow. However, the holes formed *sketches* as he drew them up.

The haggard, old man relished the time of the old kingdom statutes when the barricade was intact. When Biu kept invaders at bay. He had become the spokesperson for the court. His connections to politicians gave him influence over court systems.

The haggard, old man proceeded to the secretariat to put down notes of his finding. The secretariat looked deserted, except for a throng of people coming from the mosque on Fridays. Usually, there was relative calm on other days. Some books were being taken out of the archives to be placed in libraries where they might attract someone who got its index.

A file tagged *Meetings and Discussions* found its way among routine files in the secretariat. This chanced event would make its way across relevant desks in the office for deliberations. This was not the usual discussion being heard. It had nothing to do with routine tasks. But one eye observed it and stopped it in its track.

"May I go through the contents of that file please?" the haggard, old man asked.

The lady carrying the file stopped in her tracks and looked at the man with suspicion. Normally, such files were not routinely treated. She was going to put it in its place, having gone through the documents. Perhaps she had unknowingly given some information away. She tried to remain calm. It was her duty to report any updates to existing files. However, the contents of the document were revealing, and she wouldn't want to implicate the author. It was unlikely for it to be seen if she was cautious. *What if she planted it there?*

"Yes, you may," she replied, looking fidgety.

She silently prayed it would just be a glance. That he wouldn't scrutinise the document. This haggard-looking old man rose to high ranks of office. He represented the wealthy, corrupt class. He was an editor of the literary board. His demeanour resembled that of an officer who had fought in many battles and could thus predict plots. He got the rank of a noble and protected the interests of the political class.

"Are you alright?" he asked her.

"Yes, I am." Glad to be on duty again.

"Oh, I see. It seems so many clerks are prowling around the lobby today. Only that you were carrying a file my eye chanced on."

"A likely coincidence, as you were about your favourite spot."

"I was about to leave. What is in there? An excitement to catch up with friends at the bar?" he asked, referring to the file.

"Wouldn't know what your preferences are. Nothing unusual, I would say. I haven't seen your articles on the notice lately. That would do for some excitement."

"Never knew you were watching closely. I relish the times of the old kingdom and statutes. It seems all fading away now."

The haggard, old man was a conscript while in the military. *Had he recruited spies?* He worked in the engineering department. He wrote several articles on the causes of the breakdown of the barricade. He worked on the model alongside others to reconstruct another barricade. There were rewards associated with such excellence.

He heard about Madika's visit to the tomb and was curious to know what inspired her visit. She was unknown to him before the incident.

"Why do you think so? Would something like that jerk up excitement in you?" she asked.

"Well, the invasion at the barricade has fuelled security concerns and speculations in our security network. The holes in the walls, before the final collapse, testify to this. It seems we are being run over by aliens, hence the chance of success is little. I believe such aliens have reared their ugly heads again in the tomb."

"What do you think went wrong?"

"I think the security agents no longer receive the requisite training. Our detectives lack the requisite method of identifying this invader. That should help remember related incidents. Those that will pass this on are long gone. And the information stifled away because of a lack of documentation. These are some issues being currently raised in this secretariat. I suspect the file you are carrying may have some updates on these issues."

She seemed to know the contents. And the purpose of its circulation. However, she was taken aback by the abrupt intervention of the old man.

Looking at the front page, the haggard, old man saw illustrations of the directions of a river. It was like reading a map. The river flowed towards the tomb from the place the invasion occurred so many years ago. He realised the illustrations could suggest someone's quest.

"Who is the author?" he asked the clerk.

"Do you know something about the disruption of the tomb? Do you know about Madika? We have only a few loyalists here. Never mind my suspicion when I stopped you."

His mind quickly flashed to the spy... The old man had been wary since seeing the holes forming *sketches*. It called for caution about the implementation and construction of the barricade.

"I wouldn't know. As you know, I don't have any business there. I am a clerk here."

She was extremely fidgety now. She struggled to maintain her calm. "Sir, please, can you give me a second?" She dropped the file on a table next to the man and hurried away.

The haggard, old man lowered his spectacles and started flipping through the pages, as though looking for something in particular. The haggard, old man flipped through the papers. There were hills in the background.

He found a replica of the model of the barricade in the book. But this formed a tunnel with gushing water. There were sketches of a hill overshadowing a river, where a maiden could be seen dancing to some melodies. The river girl emerged from the pages. She was pictured dancing between two smiling crocodiles. And the one who was no other than the *bearer* was still afar off. He was trying to negotiate his way between still waters. He seemed able to bear the crocodile across his shoulders…

Could the river girl be behind the controversy at the tomb? The haggard, old man became even more curious about the author of the document. He also found a footnote: *She inspires many. One of her converts is Madika.*

Madika was inspired by the folklore of the river girl in Miringa. She followed the river girl's twists, just as in the *sketches*. The river has brought its fortunes far. Some believed the *bearer's* fortunes were directed at the barricade. But the barricade had been transformed into a tunnel from which water flowed to the villages.

There were theories and counter-theories about the significance of the river girl, as many more philosophers arose. How the scientists sought an explanation for the emergence of the river girl, but it was to no avail. As predicted, the coming of false prophets who would come to deceive men. She evaded Yamtarawala's spies but now was found by Madika.

Fanatics dissected Yamtarawala's religion and picked out and chewed its pieces. Yet they attempted to remould it back into shape. Fanatics' connection with society weakened as the river girl came out of hiding.

The haggard, old man saw a description of the markets around the villages. The exchanges that took place there. He looked at photos of the rituals happening at Tila Lake. Samples of water were drawn out in succession and taken to the palace. The residue settled beneath the waters, where cries could be heard from a hole in the pot in which it was stored.

Notes were found in the document: *To revive folklore in the market, and shape historical characters and places passed in documents. Suggestions that the bird creature transformed into the river girl. Or characteristic of her. The river girl was accepted as folklore, but the bird creature was perceived as controversial.*

The river girl emerged once the crocodile relics rose to the surface. But she disappeared almost immediately. Religious fanatics were waiting for answers. All followed Madika in hot pursuit, as she alerted the guard. This led to social unrest. Religionists protested that their place of worship had been closed.

The agitations of religionists were fuelled by a great belief in the bird creature. They believed only the bird creature could grant the bearer access to Tila Lake. There was reporting on such events in their chronological order.

Many conspiracies were underway. How did such discussions get here? The progression of events relating to Tila Lake intrigued him. He feared such conspiracies would breed fanatics. He thought fanatics had taken to publishing.

"Who could be involved in these discussions within the secretariat?" The man thought to himself.

The haggard, old man gained insight into Madika's motivation for gaining forceful entry into the tomb. And such depths she sojourned when she took glimpses of Tila Lake. It was to satisfy religious curiosity and yearnings.

He felt power was in the hands of unknown persons. His strength was failing him, or he would have done much more quizzing if he had noticed it earlier. He got off his chair, feeling perplexed. Time was of the essence. He had also spent a lot of it wondering if the clerk might return, but she was long gone. "I will see her some other time," he said. With the required resolve, he walked through the door and slipped away.

The haggard, old man heard a reshuffling of papers. He presumed that technocrats in the ministry were at work. But things do not always appear as they seem. The crocodile was rumbling again. Occasioned by men in uniforms who searched every nook and cranny for obsolete papers. The power of symbolism was evoked such that the men must reveal all true connections to the crocodile. Soon enough, there was a quake of papers, which caused the sheets in the secretariat to fly around, out of the windows into the streets. As these had become obsolete. Such ones as the haggard, old man wished remained.

Anyone curious enough to have a look picked these up. The contents revealed caused an uproar and renewed motivations. Each time this happened, they made rites only for it to happen again. It was the seasonal quake of papers. Like an outburst of information in this computer age, leading to multiple controversies. No one source is trusted—except a combination of sources for accuracy. Even then, this still left room for falsehood. The quake of the papers signalled a downturn in political activities. Politicians flipping through papers and newsroom outlets. They were sending messages about the bird creature across all media platforms.

Word spread through the court that Madika had the trademark secret of the barricade design. She might be instrumental in the construction and repair of the barricade. There was an intense search for her.

The court messenger heard rumours of the search. He was lost in his world, but did well this time to look up relevant articles in the newsroom for evidence. He located the picture in question. He learnt of her escapades and led a new life. Something triggered him, but he kept it a secret. He now changed his favourite location to avoid undue attention. He spent less time alone and found more comfort with his colleagues.

The court messenger spent most days in the court lobby and joined in the discussions of current affairs. He might soon be eligible to contest for one of the advertised positions. He had turned a new leaf and faced his career squarely. He walked, among others, unnoticed, before someone jerked him up by the collar.

The court messenger suspended security functions in the lobby. His involvement had been irregular. And keen eyes were quick to point this out.

"You have been acting strangely of late. What brings you to the lobby?"

"Am I no longer a member of this bar? I join whatever associations or groups I find appealing, at whichever time I choose. I have faithfully served this government and deserve some recognition."

"Recognition? Have you been paying your levies? You usually protest the payments, and now you want to benefit from the contributions."

"I have made useful contributions here to warrant my demand for use."

"The levies are of utmost importance before any other thing. The senior members can only recognise you thereafter."

"Is this all about money?"

"This brings back the question I asked earlier. You have boycotted us long enough for any thoughts about participation. What about the others you courted in the field?"

"Honestly, I haven't had many engagements there either. I think I have just been unsure of which career path to take. I think an endorsement will go a long way. Or if you may, provide me with a reference."

"Now you are coming back to your senses. This way then. Let me have a brief interview with you."

"I am sure you know we must have discussed the answers already," the interviewer said ironically.

"I can guarantee that I will abide by the rules."

"I am sure you know the consequences if you cannot abide by the rules."

"Definitely."

"Have you considered any pact with any other persons or bodies?"

"No. I didn't commit myself, as I was unsure of any commitments. I would have declared so to the management. I will also do well to come more often to the meetings at the bar."

"And don't forget the levies next time."

"No. I won't."

An inquiry team approached the court messenger. He was being questioned about his knowledge of Madika's motivations for her visit to the tomb. He spoke with a trembling voice as he answered the questions.

"I know nothing about her hibernation," he stated.

"But she was often seen with you in the fields."

"It was nothing romantic, just one of an acquaintance."

"Could you predict her whereabouts?"

"Why?"

"Are you aware of how she may have gained the trademark of the barricade design?"

The court messenger felt a prick in his heart. He had unwittingly allowed a spy to spy on court activities.

"I would probably guess wrong if given fair chances of two. Our meetings were probabilistic. One of fate. My attractions brought me the strangest of people. Not one I wished for. But I wished we hadn't met shortly afterwards."

"Why do you regret it now?"

"I don't regret meeting her. But I am being questioned here as if to be held accountable. Maybe I should have done things differently. But I had no suspicions of her, except for her curiosity."

"What was she curious about?"

"She seemed a scientist. One who sought evidence. She inquired about the court's architecture. What I thought of its significance. I honestly didn't have the answers she sought. Other times, she seemed someone lost in her world such that her thoughts were audible. This kept me thinking away. The life of solitude I wished for."

"You must have been friends then."

"Joined by thoughts, but we differed in ambitions. I drifted away sooner than expected, as other members of the bar will testify."

"Have you any undertakings to this effect?"

"I haven't considered one up till now. My preferences were to keep things low. And I would rather request the same from you. You have my word every time you so desire. I can always testify in person if the need arises."

"Very well then. We hope to get more information from your next visit. Our clues keep leading us back to you."

"Well, I will tell you if she walks my path again."

10

Madika appeared at the public square to give her testimony. Soon enough, she started speaking. Her speech was hallucinatory. She spoke like a witness in distress. She could not wait to tell it all. The tomb's colliding objects, she explained, trailed *sketches* behind. She took up the *sketches* and performed some conjuration to the excitement of her audience.

Now her audience listened with rapt attention. The atmosphere was charged enough, as the spy and Madika would have expected. It was no longer a secret affair between two people, but one that involved everyone.

Still in her hypnotised state, she could unearth the sketches by the mention of the children's sketches in the sand. Who would know them? Are the children messengers? Whose sketches Madika had found? Now she held the *sketches* in her hand as a tool. And sketched likely routes the *bearer* might have taken to Tila Lake as if to draw a corollary between the two sojourns. She postulated on the *bearer's* dilemma.

Once their hopes were raised at the prospect of *bearer's* re-emergence, but they were dashed again as she relapsed. But the *sketches* remained in the hearts of those who had them. To pass on to their offspring. This event marked the revival of oral traditions.

"This should no longer be about excitement," remarked someone. "She has received no known query besides agitations from supporters excited about her speech. The relevance of the *bearer's* journey to Tila Lake stays at Tila Lake. We can revisit this on a visit to the place. Is she trying to assume some authority from her sojourn? What about regard for hierarchies in place here?"

Madika continued with her speech after the interruption… "I have been through all this as a first-hand witness. Having no prior agenda but allowing fate to decide as one with a pure conscience. I, therefore, present my case with no guile or malice. I present my case not as one without regard for government authorities, but as one seeking fairness within the hierarchies."

"Fate rarely has any reference for resolve, but events and fate are intrinsically linked. I understand that some may think this unscientific, but science has nothing to prove to allow the progression of my case."

"I have been destined to be associated with the *bearer's* travails, such that I can expect the routes he may have taken as if to take responsibility for his predicament."

They could all see the sheets of paper waved in the air by another interrupter. Madika noticed the haggard, old man in the crowd was restless when he recognised her handwriting on the document. This recognition was from the sketches she drew.

The haggard, old man assumed he had come face to face with a ghost. He recalled instances of the river girl in history. Her obstruction of court activities. How she had walked into the Emir's presence—defying the orders of the guards who would have shot at her but had been ordered to uncork their guns.

The river girl had called attention to Tila Lake by her disruption. She put the guards to sleep when the barricade was besieged. He imagined her transformation following the escape from the fortress.

"*Now she stands at the court gates.*" He exclaimed in disbelief! It seemed he finally met the river girl.

"He thinks I am the one behind the publication. He confronts me here," she pointed to the haggard, old man.

"Yes, I am. I must admit…"

The haggard, old man relived the echoes from the river girl. Madika heard the words and was yet determined to give her speech. Even when she saw the troops coming for her. A well-organized army than Yamtarawala's. She wouldn't give up. She would still reel off the last words from the scroll she was holding, till it was snatched viciously away from her even as she was taken away.

Those that snatched the scroll were disgruntled elements. They wanted to cause an uprising. Interestingly, they were paid to do so by those who sought to apprehend Madika earlier. The disgruntled ones would yet trail her every move.

Here, Madika highlighted the importance of oral traditions, as she recalled instances of the undiluted forms of the *sketches* that transverse time. She reeled off the words of the scroll with such passion, just before they snatched it from her. She had this knowledge buried deep in her memory.

Madika, therefore, continued with her tale. Her persuasion. Her arguments were with more flavour than when she first started. The crowd started cheering. This caused reverberations amidst the words of the bird creature. Madika had become one with the bird creature, that it might disappear and leave her with the wrangling of the people. The people came to deliberations. Like those unaccustomed to change. She said that they neglected the sacred objects for too long. It seems this was the crux of the matter with the creature. A *change* was for the brave. It was not such a common word. The change you so earnestly desired. They drew their minds to sympathise with her predicament. She made her propaganda true in the hearts of many. She was thus vindicated.

The haggard, old man would have weighed in on Madika's case with his overbearing influence. However, the scroll had been snatched from Madika before he had the chance to speak. All that drama with Madika—he feared those positions were being threatened. Even though Madika wasn't vying for any political position.

The haggard, old man and his ilk were only interested in the votes of the people. Not the welfare of Tila Lake or social systems. Madika would have done more to expose them, but she was in custody now. Her crime: disturbing public peace and giving speeches that bred religious fanatics. This was punishable with a fine. But she had to be granted bail after due consideration.

It was a hard task for Madika. There were few willing to give her support. She would yet give a speech regarding her lone journey. Though she got some information on the *perimeter* from the court messenger, she undertook her spiritual journey alone. Was this to enable her to tell her story alone? She might have met personalities on her journey, which she referred to. Even greater personalities like the bird creature. The bird creature might be a better narrator then. Only that you don't get to see her often. She wasn't even seeing flying around. Or perching on trees. She was perceived as a flame dancing on waters— by those who underwent similar journeys to Madika's.

Madika was tagged as a fugitive whose motives were questionable. Like the bird creature, Madika opposed the continued practices of neglect in Yamtarawala's court. The derelict building symbolises so many. She pursued her motive of righting the wrongs.

She was perceived as a radical who had conspired with the court messenger to give credence to her theories and propagate her views. They were both messengers who met previously somewhere—events would make them recall where. The court messenger was only an unwilling accomplice. His training at the courts might have taught him so. He was expected to raise the alarm about Madika. But he kept this a secret, as they had developed a fondness for each other.

Madika lost all family connections, except for her acquaintances. She wasn't an outcast yet. She seized the moment while expectations were high. Those who didn't believe her speculated. They could be won over too. Like undecided voters. They eventually jumped on her train. Even though she was not there to lead them, they were not a rudderless ship.

With high hopes and beliefs, which formed common points of attachment in their hearts, they were about to get freed. They were about to sail. A ship with direction.

Madika had reconciled religious sceptics and enthusiasts towards belief in sacred objects. Just as she dared to activate the *sketches*. Interestingly, the guard only realised his duties when Madika took the *sketches*. His quest was no more about Madika than the sketches.

Although Madika was inspired by the river girl, she did not facilitate her escape. It may seem that she witnessed the river girl's escape. This she recalled at the site when the derelict buildings were crumbling down.

Technocrats had created a model of the barricade for study. However, it may have spurred the river girl to wake from the dead. The disruption was a show of the river girl's anger at the construction. The flooding of the museum displayed her displeasure. However, this was not a premeditated attack on the museum.

The *sketches* had travelled as far as the interpreter, who vanished. Madika's contacts could not be traced, either. She remembered the exchanges with the interpreter, who got the *sketches* from her. But she could not give any further information. An oath bound her. This confirmed she was a messenger. A messenger from Tila Lake. Discerning minds agreed to cooperate with her. And establish the wishes of the lake.

The rites truly began at Tila Lake. Both young and old; rich and poor proceeded to the lake in orderly procession. It was that time of the year when they required an economic boom. To compensate for the losses of previous seasons. The lake roared again as if to grant them their wishes. The *lovers* were perched at their corners—scripting experiences. *Bearers* in their robes reached out to the lake in communication.

She had relived experiences dismissed as sentiments. They feared she may awaken the bird creature—and make her threats come true—as the eyes from the crocodile relics rolled in their sockets.

Madika helped uncover some truths about the river girl. The river girl turned in the lake's direction. The undecided contemplating and now in full swing with the procession making converts of them all. Tila Lake was soon becoming a place of worship.

II

Madika moved into her fortress compulsively, even as the court messenger was no longer forthcoming. He had found a secretarial job at a law firm. The question that kept coming to her mind was Tila Lake's *perimeter*. Her focus of exploration had shifted, but it was still from the same strain of the quest.

A sense of urgency dawned on her when she caught sight of a procession leading to Tila Lake. It seemed masquerades were chanting into a groove. She never thought it would be so soon. At first, she thought it was a hunter's exploration. So, it might have been some procedure before they went for their hunting. She hid behind the trees, as she felt that was the best form of camouflage. The trees wouldn't give her away if she had good intentions. Otherwise, the masquerades would turn their search in her direction.

The birds sang from tree to tree to give tunes to the song of the procession. But it was a dirge. She wondered what could have happened. The procession continued until the last man was out of sight. She emerged from the trees, panicky. She had been spying on the procession. They moved in a line as though they had been given orders. Such orders might include what to do if they found someone lurking around the place. She had such thoughts as the procession continued, with the men bearing a crocodile above their heads. She ran away in fright!

But the crocodile was dead. Its death had been perceived from afar. Hence the procession going to locate it. It seemed the crocodile had been waiting for the men who would bear it. Madika confirmed at once that the men had been to Tila Lake. She wanted to see the court messenger immediately to report this finding.

The court messenger was one subject at the courts for years. He lived a rigid routine. A life of fear and constraint. His glimpse into the outer world was toward the end of his tenure at the court. He enjoyed his freedom now and would never return to such captivity. He once told Madika, "*This is prohibited. They would think you are a spy.*" But Madika saw nothing wrong with what she was doing. What is wrong with observing a procession from a tree? Perhaps what could be wrong may be spelt out when she was caught lurking among the trees.

She had her cross to bear. She wondered if they had crossed the *perimeter*. They sure had, as they brought back a crocodile. She would never meet them and ask questions. There was no point in investigating further. She was satisfied she saw them go there. She must have been feeling lucky. This could also motivate her to go in a similar direction. But she wouldn't think any further in that direction. If she would make it there, she had to follow in a train of a procession—the footsteps of others.

She wondered how they had crossed the *perimeter* and brought back a dead crocodile. Tila Lake must have granted their wishes. Such depths Madika had been previously when she was at the seabed. Now she transformed into her normal self and allowed someone else to proceed.

The *bearer* was the one foremost in the procession's train. At some point, he joined the train but left again before getting to Tila Lake. He had to bear this alone.

The court messenger assumed he went to look for snails, but heard cries from the hole of water. He might have been nearer to Tila Lake than Madika—when she caught sight of the procession. The court messenger could see the *perimeter*, but no further. Unknown to him, the lake positioned such persons around its periphery. Those who could just look up and see from where they were. The *bearer* was aware of this as he joined the procession. He saw concentric circles moving outwards in calls to eager persons along its periphery.

The *bearer* conducted the rites of passage for the crocodile at its death. The rites of passage involved the memories of the life lived. Such conceptions of life and death were established as one gave meaning to the other. It was what drove religions. With symbolism, we explained these concepts. These came alive when we observed the procession with the crocodile, as if it was still alive. There was no mourning. They bored the crocodile over their shoulders in some procession to mark its death. They conducted rites to ensure peace and tranquillity in the villages. These rites were also performed before the death of the crocodile. Just like all religions continued after death. It meant to teach the living what path to follow. Hence, the essence of the crocodile was even more conspicuous in death.

It was indeed a sombre moment. You could see it in their faces as the *bearer* led the way again.

The death of the crocodile had occurred. We do not know when. The crocodiles in the uniforms seemed dead but alive, as they were never forgotten. The crocodile symbol came into use after the rites of passage. Such use was to engrave memories of these rites in their hearts.

Priests could only deliberate matters relating to rites at Tila lake. They had the experience of performing the rites—and the right to inquire. Also, the priests admitted the symbols in the uniforms. But the priests seemed to have lost sight of their goal. They left the sacred relics to decay. Hence, the criticisms of such religionists who were tried as propagandists. Madika might get herself in such a mix and land in trouble.

It was therefore common to hear rumours about Tila Lake. Many had been there, but only a few had vivid memories of the place. They said: *The streams from which we fetched. Yet fetched from another, which we didn't know. The rivers bade us come when we left it. Here it comes to depart again into two when we sought for it.*

Little was known about Tila Lake when Madika checked for references to it. It was said that Biu indigenes paid homage to the lake and committed their descendants to its source. *There must be a source from which they drank to quench their thirst. But not this one without purification. One certified had to carry out rites. Many ailments varnished in such a manner.*

The crocodile was engraved on the uniforms of native authority officials to show they can solicit powers from Tila Lake. As much as the rites were done, it was so. This was no coincidence. Similarly, as Madika had seen the crocodile across the shoulders of those who bore it, it was a sign of her many adventures at Tila Lake. The crocodile symbol made the coincidence. Again, few people understood the tricks of magic. She had gone to learn magic. She was so confident that she displayed her prowess at will.

The crocodile lured one from within its *perimeter* till you were within its sight. You moved far away if you didn't want to see it. Or you might take ten steps forward and one step backward till you were face to face with it.

It guarded its territory. The *perimeter* had

become a fortress to bar strangers who came wilfully to Tila Lake. Those who were drawn solely for its pleasure to its displeasure. Bade *lovers* come near still, that they might sing its praises and draw many to it.

The crocodile was a fanatic. It gripped a prey and tumbled. You saw its many sides in lightning fashion. The strength of its grip was such that it didn't lose sight of its prey while the tumbling was going in the waters. We heard such tumbling now. It has just gone down the water with an antelope that strayed into the lake.

The crocodile was a disguise in symbolism. Hence, the crocodile also interested us, not just as an object, but in both material and spiritual forms. We heard of controversies, as some thought of it as just an object lacking the named attributes. When the crocodile was docile, it almost lost all its spiritual energies. It appeared merely as an object with a smiley face. *Lovers* of the lake were excited to see it in this form, as it displayed its many colours in the glistering waters. But for priests, their longing was its spiritual energy. This they would want to associate with.

We know of the exploits of the crocodile in the lake. What has been revealed in the waters— only the priests see. But who do they tell? The unbelieving *lovers*? Or the academics who were neck-deep in trying to resolve the controversies? The discourse on Yamtarawala's pose with the crocodile must have gained prominence in such instances. Being an explorer who wouldn't leave any stone unturned, he also seized opportunities from controversies. This had become an inspiration for him on how to resolve the dilemma between *classes*. Though the matter wasn't resolved in the proper sense, it created a political atmosphere for the revolving of the *classes*, like the tumbling of the crocodile.

The tumbling crocodile stayed dormant and slipped beneath the surface of troubled waters. When it was awakened, the water was still, and only then could it see those with burning enquires. From a distance, marked off by the *perimeter*. Hence, the *bearer* was at a loss on how to proceed on the journey.

The bird creature watched over the lake for 24 hours. Even *bearers* had prearranged meetings before visitations. The waters were no longer still, but turbulent, as we couldn't see the patterns formed by the crocodiles. The fiery bird creature that hovered around the lake replaced the *perimeter*. Its wings barely touched the waters, but to stir it. And to fly again. Its giant wings formed shadows over the lake. For *lovers*, it bade come near still. But the *lovers* would not come near. Persons who knew of the *perimeter* could come now. But Madika was far away. She had abandoned religious studies for science.

Similarly, many priests abandoned rites and became mere ceremonial figures. They now sat on their garden fronts for a passer-by to wish some greeting. They often said, *"Tila Lake is no more, and we do not know now what to do. Or what rites we may perform to appease it. The perimeter is far from us. And no longer draws us to it. I have been sitting in this chair all day in wait for some child I sent to an errand. I would smoke out some pipe for relief of some wanting of Tila Lake."*

Interestingly, these were the priests who the people looked up to for guidance. But that was in the past. Those who live in modern times want to investigate the past. But with the wrong parameters. We can only investigate what we understand. The priests do not know what rites to perform at Tila Lake. Or what rites to perform that market activities would blossom? All was left to chance and uncoordinated. They gave room for petty talk. They were engaged in one controversy—

over their proximity to Yamtarawala. Which village gave him the warmest welcome? Or who was most welcome in his courtyard, hence, which persons had the power to make laws. Such debates were frequently held even when Yamtarawala was long gone.

It was important to know the cause of the crocodile's death. In what circumstances did it die and what events led to its death? If they were natural causes, a period of mourning was considered. Otherwise, appeasement was made. The bird creature was the symbol of such appeasement. Its appearance about the *perimeter* informed of the need for appeasement. Yet the creature would not be appeased, except it was not in sight. If anyone met it while it was about Tila Lake, such a person would be instrumental to a resolve for which the appeasement was sought.

The signs of appeasement were tied to a recollection of events. The patterns formed by the crocodile were read and interpreted by persons who, like messengers, formed a chain of command. Such a chain must not be disrupted. This was because the procession to Tila Lake could not be recalled. This was usually taken seriously, as the *bearer* was quizzed to ensure he was adequately prepared. But soon enough, these requirements were waived, such that bravery or willingness to undertake the journey was all that mattered. Many *bearers* had experienced misfortunes because of the routes they followed. As a result, there were more frequent visits and processions where the subject of the investigation was brought to the palace. Be it water, crocodile, or even investigation surrounding the *bearer's* journey.

Not all went to *bearers'* processions after all. How can a few be considered *bearers* for the many? Now they even designated one called the *bearer* to Tila Lake. They said only he was qualified to carry out the task. How could they not explain what qualifications he got?

"This chap never studied religious studies, yet they say he is qualified," they reasoned among themselves.

"Does the *bearer* qualify to advise the Emir on such matters?"

"He does, but such advice is subject to the administrative court for review. This means he can't solely advise without objections. But spiritual matters ought not to be so."

They want the legal constraints taken off. The feelings of the people can be heard louder than their cries. It was believed that losing one crocodile caused a rapid loss of sacred crocodiles. The creature had been spited. This caused instability in the region, making it much less friendly to humans. Circumstances had taken them a step further, leading to even more threats from the creature.

The *bearer* took the warning seriously. Biu people felt the creature's intervention was in the distant past and unlikely to be relevant now. Village heads were reduced to ceremonial figures, leaving academics to decide crocodile matters. The people failed to recall what they knew of the crocodile. The beliefs in rites at Tila Lake were dwindling. They whipped up sentiments against the creature. And played down her demands. They took the warnings of the bird creature as a fairy tale. They considered Tila lake a sightseeing spot.

The subject of the crocodile was gradually eroded from the discourse. There was no such place for such discussions in the curriculum. These only led to confusion and general apathy towards the subject.

"Is that why the priests have become ceremonial figures?" someone asked.

"Exactly. Those who have firm beliefs in

traditions cannot act in isolation. Otherwise, they accrue the benefits alone. But the actual issues on this matter were discussed in secrecy. The *bearer* was left with his dilemma. The *bearer* reports his findings to a few well-connected people, while the rest believe the subject is not that important. Through such connections, Madika had been at the depths of the sea."

The times for the rites done at Tila Lake were struck off books as fairy tales. There were arguments and counter-arguments on its effects on the socioeconomic well-being of the people.

But Madika was a step closer to the *bearer's* connection. Her sojourn led her to unlock the potential in Tila Lake, providing access again. And the bird creature wouldn't disapprove, thus allowing some respite.

The anticipations about the *bearer's* journey were rife again in the villages. For a while, those who visited Tila Lake primarily were *lovers* who didn't have any burning enquiries. The *lovers* were pleased with the surface of the glistering water. They wouldn't understand such depths Madika journeyed to or even the *bearer's* journey.

The *bearer* continued his journey after being interrupted by the bird creature. He presumed there was still some way to go, so hastened his footsteps. He left the chants of praises, wishing him good luck as he proceeded into solitude where he communed in the depths of the water.

12

Madika observed the bird creature speed down a mound along Tila Lake's *perimeter*. "This is controlled gravitational pull," she thought. "I must find out the workings of such science, but how would I approach this creature?" She thought again. She passed there many times but didn't catch sight of the bird creature. The bird creature might have seen her too. She wasn't a strange face after all. She summoned the courage to walk up to the creature. But she could only scream from a distance.

"Hello, I saw you going down that mound with such speed. I am a scientist and I think some information on such a procedure would help me come up with some theory. I am just curious. My name is Madika."

"Well, pleased to meet you. What gives you the impression that I am expecting any visitors at this hour?"

"I don't receive any visitors either. I stay in the woods. Perhaps fate would have us meet."

"How long have you been staying in the woods? It seems you walk around this *perimeter* often. Can't you see these areas are marked off?"

"I can see the signs. I can see the workings of someone like you here. When I moved here about five years ago, they had demolished illegal structures, and I thought I should move quickly."

"Sounds scary," she joked. "Well, I don't know how to help you. What is your hypothesis?"

"The force of attraction that pulls you to the mound varies with the distance between the *perimeter* and the crocodiles."

"So, do you want to know how I developed such a force?"

"If you understand gravity so well, you are likely to develop a propelling force that makes you defy gravity. Probably that is why you developed wings." She chuckled.

"You seem to know a lot already. I would grant you an audience next time I see you."

Here she gained insight into the scientific workings of creations in Tila Lake. She sought acquaintance with the crocodile.

This was the first personal contact between Madika and the bird creature. Each read different meanings to this secret meeting. For Madika, she realised her sojourn. It could just be the beginning. The bird creature realised Madika was drawn by the *perimeter*. Impressed by her curiosity, the bird creature offered to reveal the artistic designs in Tila Lake, controlled by the mound technology.

The creature had communication lines to reach Madika. This was a trademark secret between them. If she needed her service hastily, they could communicate via the sensations that ran through an activation centre where she was domiciled. Besides, the bird creature could provide Madika with information about the events around Tila Lake, since she was in the mound most of the time.

Madika was introduced to the activation of communication lines between mounds in the lake. While Madika was on the mound, the bird creature activated the latch from the ground. Madika picked up the sensation, flew off the mound, and fell some steps forward. The bird creature laughed. "You still require some more training," she said. Madika had come several times after to continue her training. "Few people know I am doing this," Madika responded.

"Why would they have to know?" the creature replied.

The relationship continued until Madika could spring and bounce high with her legs for recreation and survival in the wild. She could bounce in leaps and cover great distances. The science of the spring in the legs was an improvised version of that on the mound. She also communicated with the creature from an activation centre, which was jointly created by both of them. Certain aspects of the workings were known to Madika. But she couldn't figure out the workings entirely. This trademark was kept secret. However, she knew of the activation centre at Tila Lake, which the creature used.

The activation centre was buried in the ground and attached to a receiver. In addition, the receivers were positioned in the mound at Tila Lake. The signals sent to the receiver sometimes meant the creature came out of the mound for a scheduled meeting. At such times, the creature will leap and rest on the mound. The latches would refuse to lock, but stayed until the creature reactivated it from the lake's centre. Then the bird creature would have to leave the mound. Madika couldn't activate the latch as the creature could.

13

The tale of Madika was prominent among so many others. She stopped by the mountains on her way from the farm. She made a tent by the mountains, then thought of a hut, somewhere to smoke some fish. A habitable place, so it was—till she drew attention from others. She got a name for herself—an alien—one alienated from the others. Yet her farms did the best, and she was joyful on market days. She soon became the subject of investigation. When others' sales were dwindling, she made off with baskets of produce for profit. Other times, she was the subject of entertainment when she came to the market square with an aura of magic. Thus, she lived between cycles. She was left alone for a while until an officer came knocking.

This one visitor came so close to the information on the whereabouts of the *bearer* as advertised by the clowns. Madika seemed knowledgeable about the *bearer's* predicament. Instead of bickering, he thought to use his offices to investigate her. He approached her, following a first line of investigation. He looked for contradictions in her statement to try her from the point of law.

She must have expected some trouble in the village centre, then was here or compelled to be there. Otherwise, why did she choose to be in the woods? This is not entirely strange. If her choice of wood decorated her house. The woods stick out of the roof panels in the heartlands. There is less need for it as you move away. Where Madika is found in her lonely edifice with thorns around. Nobody came near, making her abode suspicious.

Sketches of the Tila Lake's wooded areas could be drawn and traced just as the officer picked his way between thorns, which were used to demarcate her house. He must have come with some scratches. But how did Madika walk up here with bare feet? She sprang over the thorns with springy legs. The gift she got from the creature. Up and over, she was now on the other side, without thorns. She had the similitude of someone being looked for. She expected being taken away from here against her wish. But for another cause in which she will partake, she would agree. But the officer was away. The officer had turned away from the point of demarcation, only to return.

Garmadika was a name that resonated as you approached Waka. It described Madika's association with her mountain. The name evoked memories of her bravery. She took to harness the power of nature in such a unique style. She studied various habitats and forms of living. The fish lived in water. The bird perched on trees and made its nests for young ones. Despite the wind, the nests remained intact. A snake had consumed one egg, but the rest of the nest's contents were untouched. The earthworm burrowed in the soil to produce patterns for oxygen.

The wind was blowing from the highlands to the lowlands. Its energy could be amassed at different points and utilised. It blew and controlled evaporation and humidity. And could determine other weather indicators. The trees returned to the soil when it fell and decayed. The balance was altered when many trees were felled for firewood or other purposes. She learnt the balance of nature in no little way.

She envisaged building a fortress roundabout that no one could penetrate. An annex of the villages where she heard automobiles or running water that slipped through the walls. She stretched for straws to make herself thatches for comfort—her weaving accessories: one to write and another to sit. Indoor games were made of other materials of clay and wood, which she experimented with. She perceived nature from her little aquarium and was amazed at the survival skills of fishes. It didn't take so much. Not much space for them to do it.

She taught she wasn't doing any harm scouring in the woods. She would go up to the mountains to fetch some dew, rather than shake off those that fell on the leaves. So, she was allowed some recreation. A time to bring out the energy in her. Springing from one mountain to another, she gained the skills for recreational combat. Madika had now become an expert with such springs. She expected some other sparring partners. But other activities took up her time, like hunting and gathering. The birds scattered grain before her and brought messages from afar off.

Now that she had springy legs, she sprang to the top of the mountain, took the dew atop, and brought it to her home to make some comfort. She watched to her satisfaction, seeing the dew melt away like some candy in your mouth. Only this time, she would have to collect its water side-by-side rainwater. She developed tests to determine the chemical composition of both samples. Each varied distinctly, which was determined by atmospheric conditions. Her findings could be published on the health advisory board.

Madika developed such an interest in activities in the soil and soil cycles she was considered a soil scientist. Among her peers, none were so described. This enhanced her survival ability in her makeshift home, which was closer to nature than ever. She had developed the spring mechanism in her legs. Now she didn't require automobiles to commute, as her springy legs could take her across far distances. She could save the planet from the harmful effects of global warming. Yet she was not Greta Thunberg. She would go places if only people listened to her. She has developed an internal mechanism for dealing with global warming.

Like a cat, she was agile. One that could stretch in leaps and bounds till she was atop. Coming down in like manner. To wet her plants that sought sunlight. Their leaves were indicators of the seasons. Other improvising did she observe to make her fortress a resort.

Already many saw her gardens. She improvised water sprouts that formed a fountain of water. The branches fell off the trees and were arranged in such patterns to allow for some commuting. The branches wouldn't form a clearing—or little was done to make it so. Of the plants, she ate. Roasted yams with the peels neatly stacked up in a corner. This was preserved for other uses. Her traps caught the requisite game with little ado. Probably because of its layout. Her regular meal was rabbits. She caught wind of the events in the village by the gossip from the girls that came to the stream. Unless approached, she wouldn't interrogate them. Unless approached, she wouldn't interrogate them. Until the officer came knocking one day, she wouldn't leave the isolation of her home. He had seen the smoke coming from her house.

"Please madam, can I have some water to drink? The town is in disarray for fear of a potential explosion," he said amid mouthfuls of water. A cannonball has been set loose. It could spiral out of control any minute. She read the *times* and could expect the time for any such catastrophe. She knew of the making of such a cannonball. And fires that consume entire forests because of drought and dry winds. It only took two events to create the right timing. Previous cannonball incidents had been dissipated as soon as they were found.

It was Harmattan. The dry winds came raging. Having gathered strength from the north and south. When strong winds blew, she sat in her mud-thatched house; the winds threatened to blow off her roof. Her fortifications were strong. It would have dismantled the bricks. But no, it greased the edges, causing some creaking noise at the edges. Though battered, the house stood firm.

From her knowledge of the elements of nature, she estimated the amount of energy the cannonball might have dissipated along its paths. She estimated six such combinations and was sure the cannonball would still be found as a whole. Meanwhile, the officer was trying to eliminate unlikely paths. Other officers had also been sent in various directions so that they could come to a quick resolution. He thought to interrogate her to know if the cannonball left any trails. Any trails from other directions would have been conspicuous.

"How is it you live here?" he queried.

"I came to make a fortress out of the woods. A spiral of many magnificent designs. A hiding place away from spies and observers. I hope you

148

haven't come to spy on me. Some are spies, others observers," she replied.

Spies followed a script. And made permutations that led them to possibilities of such in all directions. The information led to targets. The officer could be a trained spy.

"I stumbled here because of the enormous number of trees, fearing this place might catch fire," she continued.

"Because of a missing, fiery cannonball?" She gave him a smirk. "I understand the *times*," she said.

"We look out for possibilities and suspects. That's the training I received."

"Am I now a suspect?"

"We know the *bearer* propelled the cannonball. We also know the *bearer* was prevented from furthering his journey because his torch went dim. He met a bird-like creature on the way."

"What has that got to do with me?"

"The regeneration of the facial construction of the bird-like creature showed a woman with deep eye sockets and a slightly broad face. We captured fleeting scenes from this encounter."

"That still doesn't tell me why you are here."

"Well, the movements recorded closely match yours when played in slow motion." The creature was known to fly and spring up at different points during the encounter. The officer looked at her features again more closely. "How do you adapt to this environment? Your abode is fenced by thorns. I saw you spring over them earlier. You must have some adaptation closely related to the bird creature."

"Is this area under surveillance? How did you get here?" Madika questioned the officer.

"Look at the far end. It has been dredged to meet a footpath. That is how I came."

"Since when did such adaptations become a crime? I am a soil scientist. I note the traits of the specimens here and analyse how they might evolve. Do you believe in Darwin's theory of evolution?"

"I am no biologist and take no such interest. Are you saying you have grown to have such adaptations? If so, we must trace your lineage from the bird creature. We have to be careful not to be run over by some aliens overnight. There is a high risk of that happening. I would also like to know if there are others having such adaptations. You said you were working on some specimens."

"You can look at my laboratory. Other scientists can verify the extent of my research. I also do not have any external collaborators."

"I will investigate such samples. You could still try to raise a conniving army," he joked.

The officer felt she was cooperative during the interview. He also got adequate information. He felt there could be other ways to curb her activities.

"As you know you are now under surveillance, I will still expect you to submit your findings to the research board. They have newsletters sent every quarter, so we would expect your contribution as often. For now, we would assume that some members of your lineage were lost in transit. You are innocent until proven guilty. Discretion is allowed here, so I will give you the benefit of the doubt. Your prying tendencies could also give clues in our search."

"You still seek clues from me?"

"All hands must be on deck at such a time. Though I do not know any of your family members, I assume you must have lived in the community for a long time."

"Why do you think so? I could have migrated here only recently."

"You have chosen here as your laboratory centre. Your relationship with the villagers must be strong enough for such commitment."

He sensed he could yet get information from her contacts. Some hunters might have provided her with some samples of the animals she had. He also knew they rarely sold such in the market.

"I go to the village square… I caught wind of the missing cannonball from the girls that came to the stream."

"This time it is collaboration. I will be discreet in reporting the outcome of this investigation to government authorities."

"What information do you seek? I intend to make footpaths with those stumbled trees lying about. I can invite people like you to come freely to my laboratory centre. You shouldn't have to bother with the thorns—or my springy legs. I always longed for springy moments in the woods. This time I will put all my expertise into use and make a fortress for my laboratory," she elaborated.

"I wasn't sure if this area would be marked off. However, I was careful not to disrupt the balance of nature here," she continued.

"Were you at the crime scene?"

"How do you mean?"

"Tila Lake was marked off after the incident with the *bearer*. Only officers could go there. Would you volunteer to come with us? Perhaps there are events you may recall?"

"I just do not know how this will work out. Your training differs from mine."

"We would work together. We are open to suggestions."

She felt she committed herself to the search. It would become even more suspicious if she declined. This would bring other allegations to light. A deal was struck. Meanwhile, the officer took down notes. He looked up from his notes.

"I will only report the obvious trespass in the marked-off area. We may also want to get some information on your technical abilities and improvising. I can assure you this will not be a criminal matter if the investigation is handled right."

"I will submit myself for further interrogation."

The officer went off again in search of the cannonball.

14

The search for the *bearer* continued. The quest for Tila Lake to be birth anew was of paramount importance. The quest: a successful outing for the *bearer*. The power to go on a successful outing was bestowed on the *bearer*. He carried out the ritual at Tila Lake. He was known to the crocodile who should guide his path. The paths he had to follow were known to both the *bearer* and his guide. Usually, a council of elders' meeting preceded the *bearer's* journey. At the event, the villagers, village heads, and a party of elders were gathered. They had been working all year to make this event successful. They had a sense of duty to Tila Lake.

All were gathered to discuss the *bearer's* journey. They were gathered to discuss the probabilistic locations of the cannonball. To ensure that they could all follow every step of the journey until he was back. The *bearer's* fate was determined regardless of the input of these elders. His preferred routes were deliberated upon, but he could end up following none of these. His guide determined his path.

The clowns set the stage for the investigations. *They discussed Madika's predicament. They favoured gossip.*

"It is unclear why the *bearer* didn't follow the paths planned out at the palace. He was just in a hurry to get to Tila Lake through any means."

"But the *bearer* was known to the crocodile, having passed the first procedure of rites."

"Yes, that is what we hear. He wouldn't have been allowed to go if he hadn't passed the test."

"But this is the tradition which others like him undertook. Why then was there a hitch in the journey?"

"Well, I think he wasn't just in the lineage of *bearers*. An untrained eye can't visualise the connecting paths of past *bearers*."

"Is that why we couldn't foresee the trouble? Are we also unaware of the procedural rites?"

"Not that. The bird-like creature didn't certify the *bearer's* entry into Tila Lake."

"The impersonator, Madika, might certify the *bearer* if he tried again." A clown laughed. "Remember, she was mistaken for the creature," he continued.

"Yes, during the fleeting scenes captured—of the bird creature and the *bearer*—by the officer."

"She thinks she can emulate the *bearer*."

"How do you mean?"

"Only the *bearer* walks to find the cannonball on the way to Tila Lake. And even the assigned *bearer* was lost in transit. She knows it is an exercise in futility. Would she be leading the officers or the officers leading her? Tila Lake accepts only the resemblance of the one tasked with the rites. The rites have been stalled. We can't get to the root of the matter except a reverse process is triggered."

"Perhaps the officers lured her to get more information."

"You may be right about that."

"They may seek evidence for something not directly related to the cannonball."

"How do you mean?"

"The spiral design of Madika's fortress shows some colluding with a *lover* of such and only serves as a model to indict them. Thus, the officer considered her suitability for the search of the cannonball."

"I think the *lover* should also join in the search, then." The clown laughed. "Madika and the *lover* would be unwilling participants, communicating their ways of escape from the search."

"Can we come up with such a proposition and establish a relationship between the two of them?"

"How would this work?"

"Well, they might work hand in hand to make this a success. It depends on them. We don't care if they succeed with this."

"We make the proposition to the investigation panel, then."

The meeting dispersed. During the break, the clowns entertained the audience. The clowns joined the panel of inquiry. Wearing their stage uniforms, they made a proposition. The clowns entertained backstage with melodies in their mouths. They gave credence to the beats drummed as before. The stage was set.

Madika was presented before everyone to speak. What might she know about the missing *bearer*? Was he missing? The officer's description of fleeting scenes. Only seen in movies, but a good script for the clowns. The clowns emerged from shadows like tales by moonlight.

"What do you know about Tila Lake?" the clowns asked Madika.

"Our fathers went to Tila Lake to perform rituals. They weren't timid. But raised their heads in excitement on completion of the rituals," Madika replied.

"You must think we are here to joke. Is that the same reason you buried your head in the woods?"

"I felt invisible. It was just to stay away."

"You had anything going on with your conscience? Any insinuation?"

"I don't believe in superstitions, yet some think I do. And want to prosecute me for that."

"What was your mission in the woods?" the officer asked her.

"I was the only one living there."

"But there were those who came from other villages to view your gardens. Some even planted crops with seedlings brought from afar. Many economic activities were going on."

"They might have crept in without my knowledge, or my gardens must have grown bigger than what I imagined."

"Did you not sell some produce on market days? You should have an account of these things." Since Madika combed the wooded areas, a method of inquiry began, from wooded area searches to marked-off areas. Her footprints formed marked-off areas. They marked off likely areas the cannonball might have circuited. Yet the cannonball traced circuits to form marked-off areas.

There could be interference if the bird creature is awoken from the centre of the gravitational charges. Though a distant possibility, that could draw the cannonball to its immediate end. There might have been such communication with the creature at the time the cannonball was being propelled. This was a secret not known but now known to all. Madika navigated the thorny parts of the woods through her adaptations.

She gained access to the wooded area out of sheer curiosity. Being a lover of Tila Lake, she once heard the flapping wings of the creature while it was out of sight. She had a view of it by chance upon her frequent visits along the perimeter of the marked-off area.

Madika was found concealed here, raising suspicion about her intentions. People were surprised to see Madika there and expected something evil to happen to her. Interestingly, nothing of such was recorded. Instead, she was comfortable going there too often. She had been left to her devices when thorns eventually locked her in, which initially appeared to be weeds. She was arrested on suspicion that she had now been living in a marked-off area. But she was in the woods. One of the wood-wing estates of Tila Lake. The missing cannonball fuelled suspicion as the search culminated in the woods. Madika was lodged secretly in the wood-wing estate designed by a lover.

A lover of such circuits might be found prowling about Tila Lake, with footprints identifiable along such routes. The lover made magnetic spins, attracting the cannonball's circuits, and abruptly bringing it to an abrupt end. Once the cannonball was trapped in a magnetic spin, the bearer lost his focus since he collided with them. And started moving in spirals.

Madika should lead the way. She had been found living in the wooded areas when a search for timed incidents was ongoing. Naturally, she would be a suspect. She might have information on possible interference with the cannonball.

A road map for incidents and investigations was drawn. The template showed descriptors for wooded and marked-off areas. These descriptors would represent incidents and investigations, respectively. An induced descriptor would shed light on surrounding areas. For example, the wooded areas around Tila Lake mark off certain areas so that we eliminate the possibility of interference from signals. Because the cannonball looped in orbits, it was important to prevent its premature exit. On the occasion of threats from the fiery creature, we feared it might spew sparks, as it may conjure within such environs. Though a distant possibility, it was taken seriously. The investigations went further to show that places of such interference could overlap with the wooded areas. Nothing was secret here.

Lovers might be excited about the extent of Tila Lake's spiral estates. A *lover* would be in his estates and be content. He had such visions. He thought of *bearers* up and down the estates. Which suitable one was unknown? But to awake from his state of stupor and hand-pick one. Perhaps the lost *bearer* might have gotten lost in Tila Lake's spirals and become a *lover*.

"It was feared that such estates would trap the cannonball, considering a combination of forces. The lost *bearer* might have collided with one spin of a *lover* and got lost in transit. We have hard facts regarding your colliding with the *bearer* as he prowled around Tila Lake. We have identified his footprints along such routes. On the 16th, May 1921, you circled in spirals with him," an officer postulated.

"My fortress in the woods is not one of the spiral estates." Madika replied.

Enter clowns. Madika whispered to the clowns on request for evidence. She explained that her fortress in the woods was to safeguard her experiments in the laboratory. She has been fleeing from prying eyes since that incident at the tomb. Though she was responsible to the bearer, she knew nothing of his whereabouts. She further explained that she was no fugitive because of any crime committed.

"I must confess. I had been planning to elope with the *lover*. We were on a collision course," Madika admitted.

I must confess I was planning my escape from the community. Madika whispered to the clowns who were backstage. To elope with a lover. This was not entirely true. But it meant she was on a collusion course with the lover. But she suspected that pleading guilty would change the course of the investigations. The clowns emerged from hiding after some deliberations.

"Are we allowed to speak on her behalf? She must be exhausted now. I suspect she is speaking under duress," the clowns suggested.

"Do we all accept she is guilty of all the charges?" the interviewer proposed.

"Her intentions aren't clear about her economic activities. Yet I wouldn't call her a criminal. I suggest we should keep her under surveillance pending the investigations," the clowns whispered to the interviewer.

"The *bearer* didn't cross my path, and neither did I see him whirling in a circus. The path he chose may have been predetermined," Madika said.

"*To elope with a lover is to be culpable of collision with the bearer. Lovers* might know the whereabouts of the missing *bearer*," said the officer.

"The *bearer* may have followed alternative routes," the clowns suggested.

"How is that?" an officer asked.

"We have been on his trail." The officers showed the clowns a sketch.

On examination of the sketch, a portrait of two *lovers* could be seen. This marked a happy ending if Madika's dream came true, as this would have brought the search for the *bearer* to a close. But the sketches formed alternative routes, showing trails of the *bearer's* footprints.

"Whose footprints are these?"

"What do you say about her collaborator?"

"Are you suggesting the *bearer* was trapped?" the clowns asked.

"It remains a possibility."

"The cannonball has left such footprints. Surely someone must have walked these paths."

"How is that? Are you looking for someone in particular?" They feigned ignorance. "I would never have imagined the *bearer* walking these paths, never mind his footprints."

"But what could have trapped the *bearer* in transit?"

15

They say it was also known that Madika disappeared from town. Now that she was back, she became a subject of investigation. She left because of the controversies. But later, her research findings were sought after. She dreamt of living in other worlds. Her peers did not take her seriously until her expedition into the wild. She studied history well and knew that she would be a reference point. History repeats itself. She expected her meeting with the bird creature would yet be investigated. Nothing was secret here. She was told that while growing up and realised its significance. Everyone heard the gossip in the village, though it might have been discussed by a few. It ignited like wildfire.

Tila Lake made all such things possible.

The footprints of past *bearers* were visible on its surface. Nobody expected the events at Tila Lake. The bird creature had been at rest for years. Madika wouldn't have become eccentric to the point of developing spring legs. But Tila Lake had been neglected—calling all these events. Weeds had become thorns. The creature had developed from something. Nobody cared what that was. Darwin's theory of evolution couldn't explain that either. Madika was just a little girl. Now one who lived in the wild!

She was known as a sojourner in the wild. One who had overcome many obstacles. A mountain was named after her, as she was fond of mountains.

Madika was energetic and like a spirit on a mission. Those who didn't know her in her heyday inquired of her. Some scientists of the day felt they had better research findings than her. After all, she lived in a little village. And you probably wouldn't have just come across any of her publications. But she left visible footprints in the sand of time.

Madika reflected on her activism in her younger days. She wondered where the haggard, old man would be now. And the old, redundant structures which were all gone. The hopes of the people on Tila Lake's rebirth were high again. Her dream was to re-create Tila Lake, which had once existed.

Madika was now 87 years old. For most of her years, she was in want of mountains. A fortress she could call home. A retreat from the towns and villages where there was music and dancing, smokes of cooking. To a place where she had to clear the trees taken up by whirlwinds and storms. Slings of mud gutted the trees—its branches. These had to be scrapped. There, she discovered thatch materials for building a hut. It wasn't long before the smoke from her cooking reached the mountain tops.

Nature was her inspiration for improvisation. She took knowledge of the seasons and believed events and directions were intrinsically related. Past events dictated future directions. If the cannonball was swirled toward Tila Lake, then such an event could be replicated—the tale of *bearers* foretold.

If rivers were used as boundaries between places, the *perimeter* was one of such causes. The creature appeared in such instances, frustrating the efforts of the *bearer*. This affected the landmarks, landscapes, historic sites, and the essence of these things. Thus inducing Tila Lake as a descriptor for marked-off places, setting the cannonball off its orbit. This provoked Madika's quest.

She sensed the bird creature must have seized the cannonball. The bird creature had sensed the entry of the cannonball into Tila Lake and seized the opportunity to stop it. Madika thought a sudden increase in temperature would activate the cannonball again and provide its way of escape. By melting its connecting wires to the creature. She knew precisely what she was about to do.

Her knowledge of history was impressive. She knew history repeated itself. Some claim history is driven by theories and philosophies, but it is the other way around. Tila Lake was the centre of all activities in Biu. References were made to the lake during festivities. She wanted history to revolve around her, so she was found at the periphery of the lake. Where she spotted the bird creature, who was the custodian of Tila Lake. They both formed an agreed method of communication. She lived all by herself. Taking up the winds that came from all directions as a breeze. She was beaten by both the sun and rain alike. She fed on the game from her traps.

How Madika grew up to understand all these things from humble beginnings. An eater of grasshoppers to one who relishes grasscutters in delicacies. Her sphere of influence wielding across all villages. That name rings a bell among the *classes*. Those in need of some recognition would mention her name with little thought. Even when they were in the pubs. But an *alangoro* would keep his cool while studying events around the village square.

Alangoro described the personae of a man being referred to by his subordinate. For everyday use, it was simply a greeting. But with such reverence to the *alangoro*. At once, you were transported to the scene where it all started. But what such greeting may be said in passing as one hurried off through the stalls? Often a boy said *alangoro* to an older adult. Or even a man to an older adult. But for a woman, it would seem that the man towered above her when she knelt to say the greeting. Nevertheless, Madika would ask for some consideration. She would want *alangoro* reserved as a title.

How did she maintain such status among *alangoros*? She thought her accomplishments were enough for such consideration. Yet she wouldn't make such a proposition in the presence of an *alangoro*. It would be discourteous. Rather, she would muse at the feeling which was gone once she got up on her knees. She commanded her respect on occasions, even when an *alangoro* watched in awe. But he was not taken aback. He would walk amidst such a place where a crowd was gathered. To leave a trail of beckons: *alangoro! alangoro!! alangoro!!!* He wasn't permitted to look from behind at those who made the beckons. But to adjust his *babariga* and continue his journey.

If he met Madika, she would still say *alangoro*, however, with some sobriety. Then the *alangoro* would call her to display her performance of magic for his pleasure. So, she might give him his full dues. He would watch her dance to the beat of drums and cymbals. She would swing among trees, showing her strength and agility. On his lap, she danced. Then he called her to quit!

Madika knew that a renowned politician was not on a par with an *alangoro*. Though he was one in his own right. Yet not one, because the politician was usually seen during the peak of political activities. Who then would know him? Except those within his circles. He yet required some introduction, then he was regarded as *alangoro* by those on the streets. But an *alangoro* solved several disputes for those on the streets— who readily made the beckons—when he passed through the next street. Again, his face was away, only responding with a wave of the hand.

An *alangoro* summoned the clowns from afar. They spiced up events with Babur intonation; with performances, they gave credence to Madika's tale. They were given their stipends accordingly. But this was behind the scenes without knowledge of Samuel. When Samuel echoed a verse, the clowns formed a chorus to drown the verse. Thus, the tale was still explainable, with the verse less significant.

Madika represented the wishes of the people as she opened up a mode of communication with the bird creature. Her laboratory was in the woods. Her exploits now sang as choruses. It was never about navigating escape routes to erase all traces of contacts when she was on the run—but that she didn't take the path of the convention. Let us examine her evil deeds, if there are any.

The clowns played one evening. They staged a woman who had been planning exile alongside her lover. The *lovers* had such lofty hopes if their dreams came true. They might lodge proceeds from their dubious dealings in foreign banks, like some lousy Nigerian politicians do. Visitors were trooping to their houses to congratulate the *lovers* on their completed estates. All the while, they watched out for spies among the people. They tried hard not to give anything away. But it seemed their expressions gave them away when someone among the crowd started talking about the *bearer* at Tila Lake.

The stage was set for more such scenes. But the script was with Samuel, who later beckoned to the lead actor.

"What is happening to our market days? Is this the new normal?" The clowns asked.

"We can foresee events before they happen because we are the clowns from afar. Though you may find this suspicious, we warn the people about the state of affairs at Tila Lake. Those that intend going into exile like that couple can do so now."

"You say suspicious? Who takes a suspicious warning seriously?"

"You may as well ignore the warnings of a serpent because you suspect its movements."

"What do we expect of the couple?"

Enter the couple with a look of uncertainty. Dressed in wrappers matching. Like one woven around the two at once. Yet in separate pieces. It seemed they were inseparable now. They must have been plotting their escape for a long time. If they had to escape, they had to jump on the same train before anyone became suspicious of their wrangled movements and attempted to separate them. They were now speaking to themselves. The clowns echoed the words: THEY ARE PLANNING THEIR ESCAPE! They exited the stage as quickly as they came.

"We know their plans now. Maybe they would conclude their exit at some convenient time during the investigation."

"How do you mean? Where would they go? The couple had been planning this for a long time and seemed to have the backing of those in high places. Before you know it, they would be readmitted to our communities."

"You made a point there. We don't know who is who these days. When Na'Allah was alive, he would fish out such people with the help of Tila Lake."

"How, if I may ask?"

"Na'Allah reserved the right to hand pick such persons and bring them forward before everyone. On one occasion, some *lovers* were caught and protested. They were singing their affinities to the lake."

"Whoever sings a song in the face of an accusation?"

"It was a song of protest meant to lure some people to them, weakening the resolve of Na'Allah or the deciding panel. The panel required a consensus before they took any decisions. That is why you find *lovers* usually have affiliations on the panel. They need to whip up enormous sentiments in their days of trial."

"Are *lovers* synonymous with mischief?"

"*Lovers* are aware of the sentiments they provoke in the people's minds. It is a route for *lovers* to escape from the present realities, even *lovers* at Tila Lake."

"I suspect those are good."

"All *lovers* are good. It depends on the sentiments they bring."

Samuel gathered all the information he got. Acting as the representative of the band. He usually worked on protocols for the band. He wanted a serious outlook on some outings. But he still needed the clowns' platform. The clowns had a reputation for brilliant performances. They were allowed snippets of interviews with politicians to cover political scenes. Samuel worked tirelessly on such a blend. Their focus was to correct the ills of society. They didn't want to be classed as mere jesters. Some of them applied as court messengers, as they felt they had the qualification to further aid active news dissemination. They gathered enough information as they went around the villages. They were also represented in every dispute. To mark the resolution of disputes, they gave performances. They learnt the communications between *classes*: a struggle for relevance. It occurred to them that most of the problems could be resolved via good communication. They tried to improve with feedback from their audience. Now the stage was set.

"Do you know the Emir requests our presence?"

"All our performances haven't gone unnoticed after all."

The Emir required such performances in his itinerary for reflections between meetings. Some things weren't clear about the *bearer's* mission at Tila Lake. Village heads gathered with their submission. The clowns watched the session to a point of resolve. They were taking notes all the time. They wrapped things up by presenting the characters from each participant. The participants were now better able to listen to themselves and reflect.

The clowns usually had opportunities to perform at court playhouses. Their performances were relevant, since they were aware of the goings on in the village. Politicians had to grant interviews to the clowns. Some politicians were worried about the performance and thereafter declined interviews. But even this was reported in the news, which was not seen in a good light. The interviewees, who were worried, now thought to set the time slots of the interviews. Because of recent developments, they approached the commissioner for culture and tourism for an interview. The aristocrats were the custodians of history: tales handed down for generations and across all social strata. With such finesse and eloquence, he has been deemed fit commissioner for culture and tourism. He wouldn't want to decline, as it was standard protocol to cover such events. Especially ones that had a direct relation to Tila Lake.

We were heading now to the exhibition house of the commissioner. We hoped to find him in good spirits. Interviews with politicians were susceptible to suspicion. There was no trusting them.

Samuel gathered his notes for the interview. He would ask questions about the commissioner's political ambitions and what motivated him to go into politics. Samuel and Co. arrived promptly at the commissioner's house. They came first to pay a courtesy visit. The commissioner had some exhibitions on display when they came in. After a while, they asked for a few minutes in private.

The exhibition was worth talking about, though that wasn't the reason for the visit. He explained the ideals behind the various artworks on display to catch the attention of his audience. Gold for gold; silver for silver; bronze for bronze; wood for wood. Each spanned different phases in history.

A collection of dislodged objects in the tomb museum was on display for the exhibition. The crocodile with smiley eyes rolling in its sockets was on display. Also, there was the craft of the *lovers'* estates. And a model of two *lovers* tangled in the estates' spirals. They finally came to terms with such realities.

The dislodged crocodile relic was put on display for the exhibition. It was built from pieces; its eyes rolling as if to show approval. The crocodile had come alive as observers watched which direction it turned to. They feared it might come after them, even as the ghosts had done to Madika when she unwittingly entered the tomb.

The exhibition was open to all. People came here seasonally to learn and get the experience of the lake. The estates were being modelled on display. People came to see the making of this architectural design.

The commissioner took a peculiar interest in his collections. His beliefs in these outweighed the rumours. He understood how rumours could fuel beliefs if unchecked. Recent events seemed to overshadow Madika's plight. The old guard had chased after her till he could do so no more.

The commissioner was well used to the clowns and knew how to quieten them. Madika had already answered her query at the court of public opinion. They shouldn't seek more information.

Several studies had been undertaken on the significance of Madika's journey to the tomb. The commissioner for culture and tourism had examined his collections for the effects of such study, to no avail.

He felt he had to attend to the sales at the exhibition, as they now showed interest in the prices.

"This crocodile relic would be nice to have in my house. It brings memories of Tila Lake," said a potential buyer.

"Imagine it emerging out of a box of rubbish you kept in one corner. Give it a good background. You can create the memories you want. It sells well for the memories."

"Ah, we can strike a bargain. I see a $2,500 price tag here."

"That's the cost of fitting memories to shape. It is worth every penny."

"If you say so."

The buyer and the seller struck a deal. Both were happy.

The clowns approached the commissioner to begin the interview.

"Please tell us about your journey towards politics," they queried.

"As you may have observed, it is long. I spent the early part of my career sourcing for these collections through government contracts. I fed my interests and met some decent people. Meanwhile, you understood the game of lobbying. I lobbied my way to get this exhibition contract."

"Is that how you lobby? We see many spectators here."

"It is lobbying between *classes*."

The clowns were familiar with the use of *classes* in such contexts.

"*This man's game is classic*," they whispered one to another.

"Your favourite classics, please."

"Guess you thought that exhibition was classic."

"Did I not say, *classes*? It is lobbying between *classes*."

"Oh, we thought as much," they chorused in pretence."

"Is politics about lobbying?"

"Not necessarily. Lobbying is engagement directed toward an agenda. It is usually to gain political advantage. It is not necessarily for exploitation of other classes or groups."

"Majority of politicians in Nigeria do not have any such principles. It is usually greed and personal ambitions that drive them."

"Well, I am of a different breed. We all have interests, but it is how we put such to use that defines us. Look at my exhibition centre—it is a product of such interest. People can come here and ask questions from the staff; they get educated. We can form a vibrant party out of the ambitious ones to drive an agenda."

"Is this a winning strategy? Few politicians can articulate such a strategy. I suspect we are being lobbied here."

"Lobbying is an everyday thing, especially in a country such as this. I do not think we should view it in a negative light."

"Diverting a group of officials towards a cause not explicitly stated—is that classified as lobbying?"

"If both factions can find a common ground, that shouldn't be viewed in a negative light."

"Well, in this case, there is no common ground."

"Regarding what?"

"Groups of officials are divided on the *lovers'* plight, between wooded areas and marked-off areas. If there is no overlap, then what is the basis for the investigation?"

"So, some people report. How will they come to such conclusions when they weren't part of the discussions? Are you saying they did not follow due process toward a resolution? The discussions might have been stalled at some point, but we were fully represented at each stage."

"Does the *bearer* follow interconnected routes to Tila Lake? The *council of finds* may push the agenda in such a direction and give credence to the *lovers'* tale," they said, pointing at the craft of the two lover models.

"I am afraid the test was carried out regarding the journey from the palace to Tila Lake. The entire burden rests on the *bearer* for him to bear."

"It is rumoured that Madika was in one of Tila Lake's estates when it was reported that the *bearer* experienced a misfortune. She must have got the space in the wooded estates because of your lobbying."

"Everybody cannot be wrong. The findings and conclusions were consistent with the facts. Except you insinuate the rumours are not true."

"You do not know about the *bearer's* connection and the sojourns of messengers," the clowns replied.

"Two *lovers* do not always have to elope to fulfil their dreams. Their destinies are different. I think you should be tried, just like Madika."

"Some think the *lovers* should not be prosecuted. Instead, they should be recruits for further investigation."

"I hope your conclusion is not hasty."

This brought to the fore the state of the *lovers'* affairs—and the officers. It would have done more to pacify religionists curious about the current developments. But what would they think of the *lovers'* magnetic spins? The thought that the *bearer* could be vulnerable to such traps did not go down well with them. They perceived this as a script well-acted by the *lovers* and the officers. The *lovers* were to blame for desecrating the lake. But how would they prove that?

16

One of the *dogari* was called to the elders. A tired emir was waiting. His crocodile strength was failing him after waiting for the *bearer* to no avail. He had to drink the water to continue his rituals. Unknown to him, there was no more glistering water in Tila Lake. Behind the scenes, the flashing points continued. They were now quite sporadic in their emergence. Conspicuously visible to a visitor approaching the palace. The *dogari* hastened his step and appeared before the elders.

"What time did the *bearer* step out exactly?" an elder asked a *dogari*.

"About 10:30 pm."

"If he doesn't start approaching in 15 minutes, send for a team of hunters alongside the men on the ground for a rescue operation. He must be brought here dead or alive before any consultations towards any remedy."

"Noted sir."

The *dogari* disappeared immediately. In 15 minutes, he summoned a dispatch team. The news reached the clowns; they were the first point of call for the dissemination of information. They got first-hand information from the court's messengers. But this was strictly for performance. The court's messengers informed them, since it was a publicity message. The whereabouts of the *bearer* were unknown, and anyone could provide useful information. They responded with a prearranged performance for the event. They argued this must be remembered and taken lightly, though it hasn't happened before. Ironically, they gave this as the reason the performance had to be made a priority.

The elders continued with their discussions.

"The *bearer* may have some difficulty, as the flashing points have not abated."

"Perhaps increasing difficulty."

"What's your take on the proposal from the clowns?" asked an emir's delegate.

"I think it could further widen the search base. Make the case for urgency."

"Interesting! Let them get on with it. We shall discuss with them parts they need to edit from their performance when this is all over."

The Emir was now tired of waiting for the *bearer's* arrival. No sooner had they concluded the meeting than they received urgent messages from the clowns' correspondence. They informed the palace of the message they received from the court's messengers. But this was already known to the palace. Discussions on the message to be disseminated to the public ensued immediately.

The discussion at the palace continued.

"There is a thin line between what happens here and what is admissible to hearing in the court of public opinion."

"Is there a strong case for the interference of signals and the *bearer* going missing? Giving publicity to this effect could be helpful."

"I agree. The clowns do the job on our behalf at such times. Clowns are a crucial part of the community... *They are the first point of call in the dissemination of such information.*"

The clowns broadcast a mixed message based on the *bearer*. They were careful to reach a wide audience. This information was also about educating the people on the rituals at Tila Lake. There were still many who took these things for granted. People had different interests. Their economic activities, which were determined at the palace, connected them.

The clowns' correspondence read thus: A man was lost trying to find his way in the woods. It was unclear how he went off on his chosen trajectory. It seemed he circled his chosen path often before losing control. If it were in a circus, we could tell straightaway why he was hanging in the balance. We haven't been able to trace his exact location since we heard his cries along the Tila Lake road. This was the path newly constructed for easy access to our marketplaces. This construction would bring other economic opportunities. It was also connected to the rituals often performed at the lake —the essence of our waiting for the bearer. So that we don't have to wait any longer than necessary, all hands must be on deck. Please be duly informed. He may walk in your midst; so be alert. Report any such suspicion.

Tila Lake was the centre of rituals, sacrifices, and visitations. At the moment, it lost its appeal. A sense of belonging was lost, creating a state of being perplexed. The lake, yearning at its edges, was now a sandy pot. The soil was hard and cracked. Weeds intertwined to form a fence roundabout. The water caved in even further. The water was now separated into different puddles. Boring through the puddles, different scenes of the past emerged: Yamtarawala stirring a puddle with a stick. Some scenes they wouldn't accept as true.

The people had come tracing where this evil emanated from. A council of elders continued to discuss why the *bearer* couldn't remember his journey to Tila Lake. A power tussle was ensured following the investigation. Pacts were broken, leading to chaos.

"We all know the *bearer's* path has been predetermined, such that his connection to the torch led him to Tila Lake," said one.

"I was at the palace at the point he lost connection. We could tell something had gone wrong. This has never happened before. He came telling us of his experience with the bird-like creature."

"What has that to do with the lost connection?"

"Everything. She warned him that proceeding with the ritual was dangerous. She was yet to be appeased. Evil had seeped in. Hence, he couldn't proceed."

"And we couldn't rectify it from here. The only option was a re-route. Something was amiss. We couldn't have expected such an event either. It was unfortunate."

Someone chipped in.

"The option of re-routing is not realistic because of the unauthorised road routes. A re-route is still likely to yield a catastrophe. You wouldn't detect unauthorised routes at the palace, and the *bearer* cannot achieve his aim by following such paths. Everything that will yield a positive outcome must have its foundation at the consensus of the people."

"Was the *bearer* aware that the problem could be with him?"

"Not necessarily. He had projected the cannonball successfully from here. Or so he thought."

"The likely option to investigate was the nature of the cannonball itself. That comes into play when all other factors are ruled out. At least you can have a headway starting from there."

"But the knowledge of such is locked up somewhere. How do we know where?"

"Yet such knowledge flows among us and can present itself on request."

"Little wonder then that Madika is now the chosen one. But we have to learn some lessons from this. This takes us back to the question of what was wrong with the *bearer*."

The *bearer* himself had recalled the jostling among the elders. He wasn't fully aware of the essence of the ritual and could not be said to be fully committed to it. Yet they all wanted him to be the *bearer*. Because they wanted first-hand information on events at Tila Lake and used such for some dubious means. They all wanted to gain relevance and power.

Someone chipped in.

"That happened when the *bearer* regained consciousness. You can't have the right *bearer* following unauthorised routes. Similarly, the right *bearer* must always follow predetermined routes. It implies two things were wrong with the journey. The right *bearer* would have sensed there was danger ahead. Because it is a quest foretold, the problem couldn't have been solved in the palace, either. The templates don't cover such scenarios."

"We were unaware of the obstacles on the way. We believed everything was done with all propriety."

If the *bearer* remembered the path he intended to follow at the palace, he wouldn't have missed the journey. The cannonball was thought to have traced the edges of the path, forming a crocodile before exiting at Tila Lake. The *bearer* was expected to arrive close to the time the cannonball exited.

An experienced *bearer* could control the number of circuits covered by the cannonball. So that the cannonball finished the circuit while he approached Tila Lake from the other end. Once the cannonball was in sight, he could control the point at which it dissolved in the lake. But the cannonball went off tangent and spiralled out of control.

The *bearer* was left to bear all the responsibilities. Walking through thick bushes, he appeared battered. Drawn by the fragrance of the plants which lined the surface of the island, and infused by it, he continued a step further. He was tempted to experiment with some of the surrounding plants and even hide in their embrace. But he was carried away by one tributary that twisted itself to the lake. To follow it, he trampled on some plants. A sense of guilt overwhelmed him, having done this. But he was about to know what had become of the cannonball. He mounted the rocks in the tributary's path, and eventually found himself on a sandy soil.

In a far distance, he heard a sickening cry. When he looked up, he saw the creature on a mound laughing and now walking up to him. He wondered why she was laughing, yet she laughed even louder and told him he needn't have come. On hearing this, he was extremely angered and sought to kill her.

In one sweep, he took out his sword and aimed for the bird creature's neck. She was too fast for him. In response, she ducked and jumped high, such that his sword could not catch her. As she landed, she taunted his sides till they ached. On a second attempt to strike her, she simply flew to her abode, screaming as she went. This was where she lay throughout the year. She had been awoken by the *bearer's* presence and had seized the opportunity to taunt him as she did to those who had come before him.

He sought to go after her again, but all such instincts left him. "What made some succeed in this bid?" he wondered.

Madika understood the signs when she approached the *perimeter* a second time. Out of the *perimeter* came the bird creature that brought it alive. She knew nothing about any signs of appeasement, only that she saw the bird creature again. But this time, she kept this knowledge to herself. She never knew that the number of lives the bird creature had were tied to the number of crocodiles in the lake. So, when that crocodile died, a part of the creature died. But this was hardly noticed, as there were about 800 crocodiles in the Lake. The creature, therefore, required an appeasement to regain its lives back again. The rituals at the lake held great importance.

Since the appeasement had not been made, the *bearer* was denied entry to the lake after crossing the *perimeter*. He intended to make requests for the people. Instead, he lost sight of his torch. Madika joined the hunt for the cannonball and discovered that the creature was at the centre of the controversy. It was too late to rescue the crocodiles. The heat Madika created from her hands melted the connecting wires of the mound. This forced the weakened creature out. To her surprise, she found Madika and a host of others waiting.

"So, we meet again. Who are these people?" the bird creature interrogated Madika as her strength failed her.

"They are my compatriots."

"You sought my help, only to come back and fight me?" She sensed that this was not a good sign.

"You are good at reading signs, but you are

wrong this time. You should know the intent of our mission. What would you say?"

"But you should know what hour to come. I have now become vengeful, seeing everyone has departed me. It is too late now to tell you how it all started."

"It means we are the ones seeking revenge, not you. You know what Tila Lake means to us."

"Need I tell you what it means to me? I am here all day and night. You come here to perform rites at your convenience. You have no regard for the *perimeter*. Now you see the essence of the *perimeter* you once sought for. No one knew you were there, but I did as I could read the signs. I chose not to kill you then. Perhaps a day such as this would not have come. On second thought, I changed my mind. Someone else might well have been adventurous. I have kept my distance all this while, as none of you know the mystery behind Tila Lake. If I didn't keep my distance, the lake would have disappeared much sooner than this. Then what you call a triumph would have been regret. There were other ways of going about this, but your instincts pushed you to investigate the missing cannonball in such a crude manner."

"How else would I have gone about this? My house was invaded after a tipoff. Unknown to me, government authorities had been on my trail. Why didn't you foresee a day such as this?"

"I had no one to hand over Tila Lake. That has caused my sadness ever since. And why I live in the mound all day. I sought a friend long before you came along. But I couldn't share this with you. You were no suitable intermediary between me and the people. Remember, humans kept no secrets. You would have desired to take over the lake and bring a battalion here if you knew my secret. It is the way of people."

"All said and done, they are here now to do to you as you wished."

"You are wrong in thinking they have such power. You understand the science of cannonball and try to use it against me. Much more you don't understand about its timing."

As she spoke, she sought to fly and crush them all in retaliation, but her giant wings started breaking. The heat had risen to peak levels. Madika had done her calculations accurately.

Madika was being sought after. She invoked the spirit behind all the prime points in the villages. Her goal was to manage the posssibility of whirlwinds while minimizing the cannonball's dissipation. She was thus optimistic about the cannonball. The whirlwinds were strong enough to roll up the cannonball.

Wherever whirlwinds were being gathered, they would dissipate their energy by flowing into the low points. At no such time were the villages gathered in such a concerted effort. Tila Lake was a resort and a source of pride. Its emergence was met with celebrations.

The heat that would have been dissipated in Tila Lake was directed at the bird creature. This amount of heat revived the cannonball. It also reached the bird creature. Tila Lake had almost dried up. Realising there was little chance of survival, the bird creature directed the remaining crocodiles out of the lake before it all dried up. As the *perimeter* was retreating, allowing the people to come close.

As the heat consumed her, fragments of her wings flew in different directions. Its head, tail, and wings. Then the cannonball gathered momentum. Its first stop was at Tila Lake, where it dissipated some of its energy. Next, it splattered out in the market square for all to see. The village was saved from a fire, but Tila Lake had disappeared.

The *bearer* continued his journey. He felt the

heat coming from a blacksmith's welding. Sparks of fire aglow. The path he must follow has been foretold. He must come to a truce with the bird creature. The gulf in the lake was widening. It erupted into two gigantic masses. Fire erupted from the divergence. Scorching heat welcomed the *bearer* as he approached. The bird creature sunk underneath and threw the sparks of fire at him. Her surrounding environment cooled while he burned. This threatened to spread to faraway lands. Even the Emir felt the heat in the palace. He gathered the heat into a fireball.

"You have been calling me all along," said she. Just then, her fragments gathered back to herself, with which she flew away.

Acknowledgements

Special thanks to the late Emir of Biu, His Royal Highness Alhaji Mai Umar Mustapha Aliyu Biu, for his warm reception when I visited the palace. The Emir requested Mr Alhaji Aliyu Gwaram provide me with notes on Biu culture. I am grateful to Mr Alhaji Gwaram for clarifications on certain aspects of Biu culture.

I really appreciate the conversations on Biu folklore I had with the late Ibrahim Hassan. These were motivating and enriching. I would also like to thank Emeka Obiegbu for his financial contribution.

Finally, special thanks to my parents, the late Dr Olugbenga Kode and Mrs Adebisi Kode, for their support and providing me with a great education.

About the Author

Tolulope Kode was inspired to write on Tila Lake during his National Youth Service Corps in Biu, Nigeria, when he visited Biu Palace. He moved to the UK for his MSc/PhD degree program. During his time in Scotland, he delved into postmodernism and history. *Tila Lake* is his first novel. He lives in Scotland.